The Land of the Golden Mountain

Books by C. Y. Lee

LOVER'S POINT

SAWBWA AND HIS SECRETARY

MADAME GOLDENFLOWER

CRIPPLE MAH AND THE NEW ORDER

THE LAND OF THE GOLDEN MOUNTAIN

C. Y. Lee

The Land

of the

Golden Mountain

Meredith Press ❦ *New York*

The Land of the Golden Mountain

1

❦   Farmer Loo died with a smile on his face in his large dark room that smelled of incense and herb medicine. Mai Mai stared at her once jolly and joke-telling father, and shivered. In spite of the smile, a dead man still looked like a dead man. She just could not believe that death was a happy occasion, as her father had so often claimed.

So Ho, her older brother, who had been young and handsome a year ago but was now thin and pale, closed the dead man's eyes. "Remember what father told us," he said. "Death is only a trip to the other world where all ancestors have a happy reunion. It is a place we all go."

Mai Mai controlled her sobs. At seventeen she would hate to die, happy occasion or not. She enjoyed this world, enjoyed having people turn and stare at her on the streets, even hungry people who should have been thinking of nothing but food.

So Ho officially entered their father's death in the family book, and marked the date as the fifteenth day of the fourth moon, 1850, the Year of the Tiger in the Great Manchu Dynasty.

During the past year the famine had killed their younger brother, then their mother; now their father. Mai Mai hated Heavenly Tranquillity, the once prosperous village, now a graveyard. All the handsome young men had left. On Hing, the buffalo boy, had gone to the North; Mooncake Quon, the young farmer, had also disappeared, driven away by the cursed famine. Although the famine was now officially over, people were still dying. Canton, the big city five miles to the north, had sold out all its coffins.

She missed Mooncake Quon. Her father had liked him. Mooncake had asked her to leave with him but she had refused because of her sick father. Now she was sorry. She should have gone. She should not have believed that death was only a pleasure trip to the other world.

Suddenly she missed Mooncake so. She had always liked him and had thought about marrying him. If she had left with him, her father would still have died with a smile on his face.

For two days So Ho scurried around making preparations for the great occasion—the funeral. First a colorful paper house arrived. It had six rooms, built of bamboo and fine rice paper, fully furnished with paper chairs and tables, plus two paper servants standing at the front gate to welcome Farmer Loo's spirit. It was to be burned at the grave.

Then So Ho engaged a Taoist priest and two Buddhist monks to conduct a seven-day service. The monks chanted and struck little bronze bells to purify Farmer Loo's soul; the Taoist priest prayed and burned written incantations to drive away evil spirits.

On the burial day, distant relatives, nineteen in all, arrived for the ceremony. The paper house and some paper money were set afire at the family burial grounds where Broken Horn, the family buffalo, grazed.

So Ho and Mai Mai kowtowed to the grave nine times; all the distant relatives three times, with the women doing some weeping after the ceremony. The amount of crying was measured according to closeness of relationship. As none of the guests was a close relative, most of the women only made the gesture of sobbing with a handkerchief over their mouths and dabbing their dry eyes a few times.

Then everybody returned to the house for the funeral feast. Although the villagers had been starving for a year, So Ho had managed to prepare an elaborate five-course dinner. There was even meat in one of the dishes—a few pieces of pork skin floating in the soapy cabbage.

It was a successful funeral. Mai Mai hoped that her

father enjoyed his new house and that his servants were good cooks.

The next morning So Ho left the house with a big bundle on his back. Was he leaving for the North, Mai Mai wondered. Curious, she followed him. So Ho went into the village pawnshop. He had sold all their farming equipment to pay the funeral expenses; now he was pawning his clothes and kitchen utensils. Mai Mai did not really mind what her brother did; it was not until Broken Horn disappeared the next day she protested.

"Broken Horn is sick," So Ho said. "Nobody cries for a water buffalo as if an ancestor had died."

"It is not sick," Mai Mai said tearfully. "You have sold it, as you have sold everything else."

"All right, I sold it!" her brother said. "I sold it to give our father some comfort in the other world. Did not everything in this house belong to him? Did he not labor all his life to feed us well until the cursed famine hit the province? Now stop this silly crying!"

For three days Mai Mai looked for Broken Horn. Every time she saw fresh meat hanging in the only butcher shop in town she felt a pain in her heart, suspecting it was Broken Horn's flesh.

"Don't waste your energy looking for Broken Horn," her brother said one evening. "I sold it to a farmer in the next village. I saw it this morning. It is well taken care of and it even has a female companion. A luxury at its age. It is a lucky old buffalo." So Ho had come home every evening with a few cups of rice, a head of cabbage, sometimes a sweet potato or two. This evening he had returned with only one sweet potato. He boiled it and gave it to Mai Mai. "Eat it," he said. "I had something on the village street."

Mai Mai obeyed.

"Do you believe me?" her brother asked.

"Believe what, So Ho?"

"That Broken Horn is happy?"

"I believe you, my brother."

So Ho smiled. Then he brought out a kitchen knife and hurried out.

"Where are you going?" Mai Mai called after him.

"Going to look for work," So Ho said, turning to the back of the house.

Mai Mai wondered why her brother went to look for work in the hills at dusk. Curious, she followed him. When So Ho reached the family burial ground he dropped to his knees and started digging weeds with his kitchen knife. He shook the dirt off the roots, stuffed them into his mouth and chewed them hungrily, like an animal.

Mai Mai watched him in horror. She almost ran to him and shared the roots with him. Blind with tears she returned to the house, cleaned the kitchen and went to bed. She thought of her brother, of Broken Horn, of Mooncake, and cried, shaking the bed with her sobs.

Ordinarily the arrival of a foreigner in a Chinese village aroused only suspicion and fear. But when the tall American with the big red beard came to Heavenly Tranquillity the villagers actually welcomed him. He had arrived with good news; he had come to recruit young men to dig gold in the Land of the Golden Mountain across the sea.

"Mai Mai," So Ho said, throwing a coolie blouse into her lap, "wear this. Disguise yourself as a coolie boy. We are going to see the foreigner."

Mai Mai would have done anything to leave Heavenly Tranquillity, even go to a foreign land disguised as a coolie boy.

Everybody in the village talked about this foreigner; nobody called him a "foreign devil." The villagers flocked to the street to sign up. Women, with their crying babies strapped on their backs, watched the red-haired foreigner at a safe distance, pointing and chatting excitedly, urging their babies to look.

There was a fight in the crowd. Someone had pulled somebody else's queue in an effort to surge ahead in the line. As a man's queue was sacred, the pigtail puller was promptly rejected from the crowd and tossed onto the street. A few men, busy as they were in getting to the foreigner's desk, even took time out to deliver a kick on the offender's behind.

Following her brother, Mai Mai was half pulled and half pushed toward the American's desk.

Sitting beside the American was a well-dressed Chinese scholar, busy entering names in his account book. The foreigner, sitting at the end of the crude table, was examining the man ahead of So Ho. He peered into the man's mouth and inspected his teeth as though he were buying a water buffalo. Mai Mai stared at him, fascinated.

She had never seen a foreigner before, although she had heard stories about "foreign devils." They were supposed to be pale-skinned monsters who grew colorful hair on their chests and arms, and ate raw meat with knives and prongs, like the ancient barbarians.

She was somewhat disappointed that this one did not live up to that image. He was almost a head taller than the Chinese scholar beside him. He wore a red shirt, a limp hat, gray trousers made of heavy cotton, and a pair of shiny boots; he was impressively armed with a revolver and a short, thick knife, plus ammunition worn on a broad leather belt.

Mai Mai wondered if there were fleas in that bushy beard. And what was in those bulging pockets? She knew that a rich Chinese would carry in his pocket a silk handkerchief, a jade piece for good luck, a snuff bottle and some toothpicks. What would a foreigner carry in his?

"Next," the American said to So Ho in bad Cantonese. So Ho stepped forward eagerly. He stood there rigidly, his bony chest out, his fists clenched, his face ashy, blue veins standing out on his neck. The American stared at him for a brief moment, his face expressionless. So Ho was the only young man in the crowd. The American did not even inspect his teeth. He nodded to the Chinese scholar and said, "Next," looking past Mai Mai.

"He's next!" So Ho said, pulling Mai Mai closer to the desk. "My brother. Fifteen. Strong like a water buffalo."

Mai Mai struck a posture like her brother's. She had strapped in her breasts and dirtied her face. For the first time in her life she wished she were big and ugly.

The American said something to the Chinese

scholar. Mai Mai held her breath, her face warm and cheeks puffed, controlling a great urge to cough.

"The foreigner says he does not hire children," the scholar said.

"He is strong!" So Ho argued. "He does a man's work on the farm. And he does not eat much." He pushed Mai Mai closer to the desk. "Please ask the foreigner to hire him. He can carry fifty catties of rice on his back without grunting."

The scholar held a brief conference with the foreigner. "No," he finally said to So Ho, shaking his head. "No children."

"He is my brother. I cannot leave him behind. . . ."

"Impossible to take him. I cannot write your name down."

"No, no!" So Ho said desperately. "Tell the foreigner my brother will work for nothing. He will do anything—sweep floors, wash rice bowls, clean boots, anything!"

"Save your wind," the Chinese scholar said impatiently. "The foreigner is not looking for servants. He is looking for hard working miners."

"Tell him I shall take half the salary and shall work twice as hard. He can put that in an agreement. I shall take only half of what I am entitled to, for the privilege of taking my brother with me. Please ask him, please!"

There was another brief conference. Mai Mai, her heart pounding, stood on her toes and took another big breath to look taller and bigger. She held the breath so long that her chest ached. For a moment she thought her lungs were ready to explode. Just as she was about to give up and cough, the conference ended. The foreigner stared at Mai Mai with a scowl, then nodded with a shrug.

"All right," the scholar said to So Ho, "he agrees to your offer. You take your brother, but you get only half the gold. It will be written in your indenture."

So Ho thanked them with repeated bows. "What is his name?" the scholar asked.

"Straw Sandal," So Ho said.

Mai Mai did not like her new name, but it was no time to argue.

"Next!" the American said in bad Cantonese. A dried-up old man who had been coughing into Mai Mai's neck stepped up anxiously. Mai Mai quickly made room for him. This time the foreigner did not even bother to scowl. He just pointed at the villager behind the old man and barked, "Next!"

2

The four strangers in the little sampan introduced themselves. The fat one with the short chin was Old Wong, the butcher; Mr. Ling, hiding his bony hands in the sleeves of his threadbare silk gown, was the schoolteacher; Chopstick Lew, a farmer with long cat whiskers, blinked and wrinkled his nose as though he were about to sneeze but could not. Four-eyed Dog Chow, another farmer, was the talkative one. When he talked his large Adam's apple bobbed.

It was early morning. Mai Mai sat behind her

brother on the bow trying to avoid these men. She was glad she did not know any of them; they must have come from a distant village. She had hoped to share the sampan with some handsome young men; now she decided to switch her interest from young men to something else. She did not know what it would be but anything would be more interesting than these four men. She had been unhappy about her getup—shabby and dirty, her coolie blouse a few sizes too large. Now she didn't care. Nobody paid any attention to her anyway, except Mr. Ling, who glanced at her with a frown, obviously disapproving of her appearance. If he frowned at her again, she decided to frown back. And she wished Chopstick Lew would make up his mind and sneeze.

The Pearl River looked muddier than ever. Four-eyed Dog volunteered the theory that the dragon king at the bottom was disturbed by the foreign ship and was wriggling with uneasiness.

The foreign ship anchored in the middle of the river was indeed awe-inspiring. Mai Mai stared at it, fascinated by its turquoise hull, its enormous white masts with neatly folded sails and the shiny railings. The sampan that carried them to the ship wobbled beside it like a little water bug.

Following her brother, she climbed up the rope ladder to the ship and joined a large group of other coolies squatting on the deck near the stern. There were about a hundred of them, all wearing long queues with the front parts of their heads clean-shaven. Two wore faded silk gowns, like Mr. Ling. One was even dressed in an old satin ceremonial gown like a Mandarin, as though the day of departure for a foreign land was a sacred occasion.

Most of the men were quiet, looking apprehensive. Mai Mai squatted behind her brother, who greeted the others near him with a nod and a smile. The sun was rising, but it did not warm up the chilly morning. Although smiling, So Ho perspired. Mai Mai stared at his back, wondering why he was quivering. Was he excited? Or running a fever? Presently another sampan arrived and eight more men climbed up. One of them, a bright-eyed boy of about twelve, carrying a bundle on his back, squatted behind a muscular man who looked like his father. Mai Mai was glad to see a boy so young. He reminded her of her younger brother who had died of dysentery during the famine. Like her brother, this boy also had a mischievous glint in his eyes; he looked as though he would be delighted to pull anybody's queue if it were not for years of family discipline that securely chained his hands and feet.

So Ho coughed, his body convulsed, his blouse wet with perspiration. Mai Mai felt his forehead. He was running a fever.

"I am all right," So Ho said. "Do you see that boy over there?"

"Yes, my brother."

"Go make friends with him. You will have a companion on this trip. Here, I have some roasted melon seeds. Go offer him some." He dug a little parcel out of his pocket and gave it to Mai Mai.

Ignoring the stares of the other coolies, Mai Mai went to the boy and sat beside him. She opened the parcel of watermelon seeds and offered him a handful. The boy looked at his father for approval. "Take it," Mai Mai urged. "This is my last parcel. You can't buy watermelon seeds in a foreign land."

The boy accepted the seeds eagerly.

"How old are you, little brother?" Mai Mai asked.

"Sixteen."

"You don't look sixteen."

"I am sixteen!" the boy protested.

"What's your name?"

"Longevity. What's yours?"

"Straw Sandal."

"That's not a very pretty name."

"I like it. You are not so big for your age."

"How do you know? I'm squatting." He peered at Mai Mai as though he didn't like her dirty face.

They ate the watermelon seeds quietly for a moment. Mai Mai cracked the shells between her teeth and extracted the little meats with her white even teeth dexterously. Longevity, having not yet learned how to eat melon seeds like an adult, pulled the meats out of the shells with his fingers. Mai Mai looked at him, amused, knowing that the boy must have lied about his age by at least four years.

She decided to tease him a little. "You are no bigger than my younger brother, who is only twelve. Nothing grows fast in him except his ears."

"Where is he?"

"I could have brought him with me if he were a little taller. Have you met people with big ears? The village fortuneteller says wind-catching ears are a blessing. They indicate prosperity. I told the foreigner my brother would be lucky in digging gold, but the foreigner only laughed, saying that if my brother had a long nose that could smell gold he would hire him. What age did you lie?"

"I did not lie!"

"How did your father make the foreigner hire you?"

"You don't look so big yourself. How did you make him hire you?"

"I stood on my toes."

"I didn't. I'm tall. I'm taller and bigger than you."

"Shall we stand up and see?"

"Why should I? Why do you call yourself Straw Sandal?"

"I make straw sandals."

"My father builds houses but he doesn't call himself House."

"What is your father's name?"

"Ta Ming. Wish I could crack melon seeds like you." Longevity watched Mai Mai's active tongue, which darted in and out of her mouth as she extracted the kernels from the shells with her teeth.

"Where are you from, Longevity?"

"Canton."

Mai Mai glanced at Longevity's father, who was now busy talking to the man on his right. Ta Ming was a handsome man. She wondered how old he was. "Where is your mother?" she asked.

"Dead."

"Do you want another mother, Longevity?"

"No."

"A devoted little one, eh? But don't be disappointed when your father takes another wife. When he comes home from the foreign land with his pockets full of gold, the first one to visit him will be the village go-between. Who would not marry him? Good looks, wealth, plus a ready-made son like you." Mai Mai cast Ta Ming another glance. "How old is he?"

"Thirty."

Mai Mai wished he were ten years younger, or she ten years older. She liked his strong features—straight nose, thick black eyebrows and prominent jaw.

"My father reads and writes," Longevity said. "What does your father do?"

"He just moved into a new house with two servants."

"A rich man?"

"Now he is."

"How did he make his money?"

"He inherited it."

"Then why are you so poor?"

Mai Mai turned her eyes up; she wasn't prepared to answer this question. Suddenly she saw a foreigner in a white uniform coming toward them, followed by the scholarly Chinese, who was limping a little. She nudged Longevity and told him to keep quiet.

The foreigner scanned the coolies, his red face stern, then he spoke in a loud rough voice. The Chinese scholar interpreted for him. "I'm Mr. Wilson," the foreigner said, "the first mate of the ship. Before we sail I want all of you to know the rules. First, keep the deck clean. Absolutely no cooking allowed. Meals will be served twice a day—ten in the morning and five in the evening. The deck is your bed. Use your own bedding, but pack it in the morning. Nobody is allowed upstairs. The washroom is at the bow. Follow the arrow and the Chinese sign. If anyone feels sick, rush to the stern; if you must throw up, make sure everything goes into the ocean. . . ."

At this point Mr. Wilson stopped and pointed a finger at Longevity and said something angrily. Mai Mai almost jumped out of her skin. "You there," the Chinese scholar translated, "stop dropping melon seeds on the deck! Clean that up!"

Longevity stared at the foreigner, petrified with fear. His father quickly apologized to Mr. Wilson in Cantonese, then turned to the boy and ordered loudly, "Clean that up, quickly!"

"If you litter the deck again," Mr. Wilson said, "you will clean the whole deck with a mop and a bucket. Do you hear, boy?"

"Say yes, Longevity," his father ordered.

Longevity opened his mouth but no voice came out.

"Yes, sir," his father answered for him.

"I'm not asking you," Mr. Wilson shouted. "Let the boy speak. Do you hear me, boy?"

Longevity struggled with his tongue for a brief moment. Finally he squeaked, "Y—yes, sir!"

"That's all," Mr. Wilson said. He turned away, climbed up the stairs and disappeared. The scholarly Chinese limped after him, his long pigtail flapping in the wind.

Mai Mai felt bad about the incident. "I'm going to tell the foreigners it's all my fault."

"Why should you?" Longevity said. "I dropped the shells on the deck."

Four-eyed Dog, who always enjoyed somebody else's unpleasant experience, sauntered over with a big smile. "Good boy," he said to Longevity. "Always answer the foreigners like a man. Tell them you are a proud Chinese wearing a queue. That will show them. Here, have a pill." He opened a pillbox and offered Longevity a black pill. "Called Snake Heart Pill. Prevents seasickness, dizzy spells, headaches of all kinds. It smells a little like old ham, but it's the scent of an herb. Here, give one to your father. I like him. He answered the foreigners like a man."

Longevity looked for his father, but he had gone to the stern.

"Heavens," Four-eyed Dog went on, "is he sick already? Here, give him two."

Ta Ming, carrying a mop and a bucket, his face grim, returned from the stern. He came to Longevity and dumped the bucket on the deck and thrust the mop into Longevity's hand. "Clean the deck," he ordered. "And clean it well. I don't want you to lose face for me in front of the foreigners."

Longevity gave his father the pills.

Ta Ming tossed them overboard. "After you have finished cleaning the stern, go clean the bow too. Give the foreigners a good impression. And don't swallow pills that every Cheong Sam or Lee Su gives you. That goes for watermelon seeds, too!" He cast Mai Mai an accusing glance. She made a face at him and returned to her brother. "All handsome men are sour turnips," she thought.

The sun was high and hot. Hunger gnawed at her

vitals. So Ho was lying on his back, sweating, his face grimacing. Mai Mai wiped his perspiration. "What's wrong, So Ho?"

"Don't worry about me," So Ho said. "How did you make out with that boy?"

"I got him in trouble. His father ordered him to clean the whole ship. Are you in pain, my brother?"

"I am all right. Go help that boy. You need a companion on this trip."

Perspiration poured down Longevity's red, hot face as he mopped the deck. "All caused by that dirty-faced boy," he thought. His mouth still tasted the fragrance of the roasted watermelon seeds. He wished he had accepted a larger handful. He glanced at Mai Mai, who was coming toward him. He decided not to have anything more to do with her.

"Look at your face, little brother," Mai Mai said. "Red as a monkey's behind. You need help, I suppose."

"I don't need any help."

"I might help if you stop looking like a monkey suffering from a toothache."

"Why should I?"

"Because it is not friendly."

"I don't need your help."

"Stubborn, eh? You shared my watermelon seeds and I want to share your mopping. And there is nothing you can do about it."

"My father won't allow it."

"He is a mean, selfish tyrant."

"You go tell him."

"I will." She grabbed the mop and bucket and started mopping the deck. Longevity, looking a little cowed, went back to his father.

When Mai Mai finished cleaning the stern, she carried the bucket and the mop to the front part of the ship. She was curious about the foreign ship and was glad to have the opportunity to explore it a little.

She saw several signs. One of them was written in Chinese with an arrow pointing to a certain door. "It must be the washroom," she thought.

She passed the signs and the washroom. Hardly had she walked ten more paces than a foreigner in a white uniform came toward her. She plastered herself against the railing to let the foreigner pass. She had learned to fear any man in a uniform. Such a man, she had been told, represented authority and controlled the lives of those in ordinary clothes.

The foreigner squeezed by without so much as casting her a glance. But suddenly he stopped and roared, "Where d'you think you're going, boy?"

Mai Mai stopped, dumbfounded, afraid to move. The foreigner grabbed her by the arm. "Come with me," he said, forcing her toward a door that led into a hot dark room that looked like a kitchen. Several men, stripped to the waist, were busy feeding chopped wood into a stove, slicing meat and vegetables and stacking up tin plates. Perspiration crept down their bare backs.

The foreigner shouted into the room, "Hey, Ah Hing, come up here!"

A fat Chinese came to the door wiping his wet forehead with the back of his hand. "Yes, Mr. Benson?"

"Ask this boy what the devil he is doing here!"

Ah Hing translated. Mai Mai, stammering, explained that she was trying to clean the ship.

As soon as Ah Hing finished translating, Mr. Benson grabbed her again, this time by her collar. "Come with me, boy," he said, half lifting and half pushing her toward a hallway. At the end of the hallway Mr. Benson opened a thick door with a small iron-barred window in it. He tossed her in, then slammed the door shut and locked it.

The dark, bare cubicle was hot and smelly. For a moment Mai Mai did not know what to do. She looked through the small iron-barred window and hoped that her brother would come to rescue her. She could see nothing but a blank wooden wall. In the back there was a small porthole through which she had a glimpse of the muddy river reflecting the bright sunlight.

She stood in the dark cabin for almost an hour, fidgeting uncomfortably. Many times she tried to sit down but the floor was damp and dirty. Besides, she was afraid to sit or squat for fear of violating another rule. She wondered what wrong she had done.

The ship moved. She looked through the window and the porthole again and saw trees and huts on the bank moving by slowly. Suddenly she heard some heavy footsteps. A Chinese seaman appeared at the window, scowled at her through the iron bars. Then there was a click and the door opened.

"All right, get out," the seaman said in Cantonese. "Next time you want to steal, think of a better alibi. Cleaning the ship, indeed!"

"I didn't steal," Mai Mai protested.

"You are lucky you got caught before you had stolen anything," the Chinese said. "If you were caught in the act, it would be the bullwhip. Twenty lashes can take the skin off your bottom and you won't be able to sit down for six months."

When Mai Mai returned to the deck, wronged and full of hurt feelings, her brother avoided looking at her, his face pale and grim. Mai Mai squatted down gingerly, waiting for her brother to speak, but So Ho sat with his arms resting on his knees, staring at the deck morosely, sweat pouring down his face.

"My brother," Mai Mai finally said, "I did not steal."

So Ho did not stir; he closed his eyes and nodded as if about to cry.

The ship began to rock a little. A few seagulls were following and circling around the enormous sails which were white and graceful, shining and bright in the sun. In the distance Mai Mai could see the blue ocean.

3

As the ship came out of the Pearl River estuary, more seagulls joined the journey. Mai Mai felt the slashing wind and occasional spray of cold sea water. She shielded her brother from the wind and covered him with a cotton padded coat. Four-eyed Dog, awakened by the roar of the ocean, grinned at Mai Mai and quickly took another Snake Heart Pill.

"Sit up, sit up!" a man shouted in Cantonese. Mai Mai turned and looked. It was Ah Hing, coming with a large bucket of food. Following him was another Chinese, who carried a stack of tin plates and a basket of bread.

The men all sat up quickly, some smacking their lips in anticipation of food. Ah Hing put the heavy bucket down, rested his hands on his lips, his legs apart, and gave a speech like a sergeant: "Every man take a plate and two slices of bread. Two slices, no more. Don't waste any, for you won't see another crumb until morning. You can eat your salted eggs and preserved beancake secretly. I shall be blind, but don't let the foreigners catch you. They say these foods stink up the ship. This is a foreign ship and you eat what foreigners do! All right, pass the plates."

While the other man was passing out the tin plates and bread, Ah Hing picked up his bucket and started ladling out a thick brownish gravy with some chicken in it. Starved by years of famine, they ate the foreign food with their best table manners—smacking their lips and sucking in deep breaths to show their appreciation.

So Ho, who had managed to sit up, took a spoonful of the food and put the tin plate down.

"You must eat, my brother," Mai Mai said. "There will be no more meal till tomorrow."

"You eat mine," So Ho said. "I'm not hungry."

"Shall I ask that man to give you a pill?" she asked, gesturing at Four-eyed Dog, who was chewing and belching with his mouth closed, his eyes slightly crossed.

So Ho cast a glance at Four-eyed Dog and quickly lay down again. "Don't worry about me. I'm all right."

Mai Mai ate her dinner quietly, her head down. Suddenly her brother half raised himself and touched her lightly on the arm. "Eat like a man," he whispered.

Remembering that she was Straw Sandal, Mai Mai smacked her lips, sucked in deep breaths and made other noises by clanking her spoon against her plate. She became such a sloppy eater that Mr. Ling, who squatted not too far away from her, glared at her and shook his head with a sigh.

"The foreigner!" someone said. A few men straightened up and began to eat with more noise to show their deep appreciation. Mai Mai turned and saw the tall American with the big red beard—the one who had recruited her—come down a steep staircase. He came to the men with big strides, his shiny boots squeaking. The scholarly Chinese who had interpreted for him before followed him closely.

The big foreigner scanned the Chinese for a moment, his deep-set eyes sharp and bright, his mouth closed into a straight line. "How do you do?" he finally said in Cantonese with a heavy accent.

"This is Mr. Carnahan," the Chinese scholar said. "He is your employer. He is paying for your food and passage to the Land of the Golden Mountain, so eat as much as you can."

Mr. Carnahan nodded with a smile as if he approved of what the scholar had said, then he bent down and examined a few Chinese nearest to him. "I remember you," he said, then turned to the scholar and asked, "Quon, where are the coolies you recruited in the other village?"

"All mixed up," the scholar said. "They all look alike."

"Not to me," Carnahan said, going around and giving the men a close inspection. "I'm not too happy with their looks and complexions."

"Most of them have lean muscles hidden under their loose blouses, which should be easily filled out after a few weeks of greasy food on this ship."

"Hey, Ah Hing," Carnahan ordered, "give these men an extra helping of whatever you're serving. Be generous with that gravy."

"Yes, sir," Ah Hing said, going around and dishing out more food.

"That's right!" Carnahan shouted jokingly. "Tell your captain that whatever these men gain I'll pay him freight for the extra weight."

"Yes, sir!" Ah Hing said, and smilingly dumped a large spoonful of the greasy food on Four-eyed Dog's plate. Four-eyed Dog stared at it cross-eyed and belched.

Mr. Carnahan noticed the men in ceremonial gowns and scowled. "What's that? A bunch of Mandarins?"

"They are proper and superstitious people," Quon said. "Such qualities are well suited to the rough gold mines. They won't get into trouble."

Carnahan felt one of the men's muscles. "Bones and skin. Ah Hing, more chicken here. And lots of gravy!" Then he spotted Longevity, who was eating his chicken dinner faster than anyone else. His scowl deepened. "Quon, you've signed this one on account of his good appetite, I suppose."

"His father is paying for his keep," Quon said.

"Where are the lean muscles you mentioned?" Carnahan said, going around and feeling some of the men's muscles. Many expanded their chests to look strong.

Mai Mai didn't want this big foreigner to touch her. Before he came near her she decided to sneak away and hide in the washroom for a little while. Besides, she was thirsty.

There was plenty of water in the small, dirty washroom. For a whole year she had never even had enough water to drink, let alone to wash. She dashed to one of the buckets and thrust her hands into it. She let the water run through her fingers as though it were jewels. Then she took off her blouse and sprinkled water on her face and skin, savoring with great delight the touch of precious cool clean water.

Suddenly the door opened and Longevity burst in. Instinctively Mai Mai grabbed her blouse and threw it over her bosom. Surprised, Longevity started to withdraw. Mai Mai grabbed him, pulled him back and shut the door. "You won't tell, will you?" she asked.

"What will you give me for not telling?"

"Gold. Half of what I'm going to earn from that big foreigner."

"Do you have salted fish?"

"No. But I have more watermelon seeds."

"All your watermelon seeds."

Holding her blouse tight against herself, Mai Mai found her pocket, brought out the unfinished parcel of watermelon seeds and gave it to Longevity. "What don't you want me to tell?" Longevity asked.

"Can't you see?"

"I see you are taking a bath. Go ahead, I won't tell."

After Longevity had gone Mai Mai was sorry that

she had given all her fragrant watermelon seeds to the boy. She was surprised that Longevity still couldn't tell a boy from a girl. Perhaps he had not seen her body. Perhaps he pretended that he didn't know the difference.

When she returned to the open deck, worrying, Mr. Carnahan and Mr. Quon had left. The ship rocked a little more now and she felt slight nausea. A few men were taking hasty trips to the stern. Mr. Ling and many others had stopped eating altogether. A few were belching. Longevity, his back turned to his father, was cracking watermelon seeds secretly. Ta Ming was eating his food without expression on his handsome face, chewing the foreign bread deliberately; he didn't seem to notice what he was eating. Old Wong, the butcher, was opening a jar of preserved beancake, casting furtive glances to his right and left. Four-eyed Dog, who had for the first time stopped talking, was cracking a salted egg under his coolie hat. Quite a few men were still able to eat their food heartily, scraping their tin plates with their spoons and smacking their lips noisily.

As the dinner progressed, more villagers took trips to the stern. Mai Mai finished her food. The foreign bread was hard and sour, but it was not nearly so hard to swallow as some of the food she had eaten during the famine. She put her brother's food into a tin can and wrapped his bread in a piece of paper. She wondered if her brother had fallen asleep. She watched him for a moment. Sweat stood on his forehead, a few drops were creeping down. She wiped his face gently with a handkerchief and then fanned him with a piece of paper. He stirred briefly, his face twisted as if a sudden pain had shot through him. "My brother," she called softly, "are you uncomfortable?"

So Ho remained silent for a moment. Suddenly he turned away with a sigh, his brows knitted. Mai Mai wondered what was going through his mind. "My brother," she asked, "what worries you so? Please tell me!"

"I am all right," So Ho said without opening his eyes. "I am not worried."

Mai Mai did not know what to believe. If her brother had shown a little emotion, or his eyes had opened and indicated a flicker of smile in them, she would have been relieved. Now she became worried herself. She remained worried and unhappy until her brother turned his head toward her slightly. "Mai Mai," he said, his eyes still closed, "go make friends with that boy. His father is a good man. He will take care of you."

"We will take care of each other, my brother," Mai Mai said.

"When I'm sick you need someone else to take care of you!"

"You will not always be sick. I will see that you get well." She wiped his forehead again and poured a cup of water for him from a gourd that they had brought.

After So Ho finished the water, he lay down again and urged Mai Mai to have a visit with Longevity.

She went and sat beside Longevity. She smiled at him but the boy turned away from her. He ate the watermelon seeds quietly for a moment. She felt like pinching the boy's ears. "Your father told you not to eat my watermelon seeds," she said. "Why are you eating them?"

"Because I like them," Longevity said.

"Don't you make your father angry?"

"He is looking the other way."

"He spoils you, doesn't he?"

Longevity kept quiet.

"If I were your father," Mai Mai went on, "I would spank you good and hard for disobeying my wishes."

"Who wants you to be my father? You are not much older than me, and not even bigger!"

"Did you say you are twelve?"

"I didn't say that. You said that."

"How old are you?"

"Seventeen."

"You said sixteen earlier."

"I'm growing."

"How old did you say your father was?"

"Thirty."

"Did he become a father when he was fourteen?"

"Yes."

"I don't believe it."

"As you like."

"A man cannot become a father until he is at least eighteen."

"How do you know?"

"Because . . . because . . . well, you are too young to understand."

"My father says to thank you."

"For what?"

"For offering to clean the deck," Longevity said.

31

"They shut me up in a dark room for an hour."

"It is all right now. My father went upstairs and talked to the foreigners."

"I did not try to steal. Do you believe me?"

"I believe you. Your brother. Is he sick?"

"He will be all right. He likes you, Longevity."

"Here, have some watermelon seeds," Longevity said, offering her the parcel.

They ate watermelon seeds quietly for a moment. "My brother likes your father, too," Mai Mai said.

"Your brother is so skinny."

"A year ago he was the most handsome man in Heavenly Tranquillity."

"He isn't so handsome now," Longevity said. "Did you notice something?"

"What?"

"The seagulls are all gone."

Mai Mai noticed that the wind had subsided too, but the ship rocked just as much. The roar of the sea was still frightening; the speck of distant land had disappeared, engulfed by the darkness of the ocean.

"So you took a bath," Longevity said.

"Yes I did," Mai Mai said, wondering if Longevity knew she was a woman. "I did not waste any water. The foreigners won't mind. If you want to tell, go ahead."

"Did you forget something?"

Mai Mai's heart jumped. Yes, he knew; he was trying to blackmail her now. "What?" she asked.

"You forgot to wash your face," Longevity said.

4

❦ Next morning Mai Mai awakened with a start.
She could hardly believe that she had been sleeping on a
foreign ship that was carrying her off to an unknown
foreign land. Her brother was still asleep. She was
glad. During the night he had slept restlessly. Mai Mai
had heard him get up, drink water and groan softly;
twice she had asked him if there was anything she could
do for him but he had said no; he had ordered her to go
back to sleep.

Mai Mai had also heard quite a few men snoring.

Four-eyed Dog's snore was the loudest and the most colorful; he snarled, whistled, grunted, smacked his lips and made other peculiar noises in his throat. It had been funny at first and she had to control herself to keep from giggling aloud. Later, when she was tired, it had become very annoying.

She looked around. Many had already got up, and were braiding their long pigtails. She went to the railing, and breathed deeply the fresh ocean air. The ship rocked only slightly on the calm sea, which stretched away endlessly in all directions. There was not a speck of land anywhere. She watched the blue water, fascinated, wondering how deep the ocean was and if there was a dragon king living down below.

Longevity came to the railing and stood beside her. "Did you see a fish?" he asked.

"No. Did you?"

"There is one now. Look."

A flying fish had just leaped out and dived back into the water. "I never saw a fish like that before," Mai Mai said.

"It's a bird fish," Longevity said. "Have you ever seen a whale?"

"No. What is it?"

"It's a volcano fish. It's as big as a mountain, spitting water like a volcano."

"I don't believe it. Did you see one?"

"My father saw one when he went to sea, years ago."

"I still don't believe it," Mai Mai said. "No fish is as big as a mountain."

"But you just saw a fish that could fly. If I'd told you

that you wouldn't have believed it either. Do you believe in the dragon king?"

"Yes."

"Did you ever see a dragon king?"

"The dragon king is the king of the ocean and the rivers. It will not allow itself to be seen so easily. Have you ever seen the Emperor? Certainly not. Nobody can see the Emperor except ministers and generals."

"Look, another bird fish!" Longevity cried excitedly. "Another, another!"

"Well, well, I can see you boys are early," Four-eyed Dog said, sauntering to them with an earnest look, his large Adam's apple bobbing.

"You are early yourself," Longevity said.

"Couldn't sleep a wink," Four-eyed Dog said. "So many people snored. They should take Snake Heart Pills. The medicine will keep people from snoring. *Wei,* Straw Sandal, what happened to you yesterday? All of a sudden you disappeared. A foreigner came and talked to your brother. I couldn't hear a word that they said. If you were a girl, I would have suspected that your brother had sold you to the foreigners as a slave."

Mai Mai's heart almost jumped to her mouth. Did Four-eyed Dog know she was a girl? She glanced at him; he was looking at her earnestly, waiting for an answer. "What happened to you? Speak up!" he urged.

"They kept me in a nice room for a while," she said. "What for?"

"None of your business."

"They thought you tried to steal, didn't they?"

"I did not steal. You believe me, don't you?"

"Well, that's not up to me to decide."

"He did not steal!" Longevity said. "I believe him! My father believes him. My father told the foreigners so."

"Let me tell you something," Four-eyed Dog said, waving a finger at Mai Mai and spraying saliva, "the moment I heard you say you wanted to clean the whole ship with mop and water, I said to myself, uh, uh, somebody is going to step into a cauldron of boiling oil. Have you heard the story about the man who buried thirty taels of gold for safety? Have you heard of it? Speak up."

"No," Mai Mai said.

"He was afraid somebody might steal the gold, so he buried it and put up a sign saying 'No thirty taels of gold is buried here.' The next day the gold was stolen. Now you, a passenger, are not required to wash the rice bowls or mop the deck. All they ask of you is not to dirty the ship. Suddenly you take a mop and a bucket and go around cleaning the whole ship for nothing. Who would not suspect that you have other designs? Look at me, I go everywhere on this ship. I walk with my chest out and my head high. I don't even greet the foreigners. What happens? They don't suspect me of anything. They even step aside to let me pass. I could steal this ship right from under their noses and they wouldn't know it."

"I didn't steal anything!" Mai Mai protested.

"I did not say you have stolen anything. All I'm saying is that you should not put a sign saying 'There is no thirty taels of gold buried here.' The sign arouses suspicion, understand?"

36

"I did not put up any sign saying anything," Mai Mai said.

"I know, I know," Four-eyed Dog said patiently. "I'm only drawing a picture for comparison. . . ."

Four-eyed Dog kept talking. Mai Mai did not know what he was talking about. She looked at the sea and wondered again how deep it was and what creatures lived down below. Longevity was fidgeting. When he saw his father coming toward them he quickly left the railing to meet him. But his father walked past him and came to Mai Mai. "Straw Sandal," he said, his heavy brows knitted in worry, "your brother is very ill. Go help him to the washroom. I'll go and find out if there is a doctor on this ship."

Mai Mai rushed to her brother, who was twisting in pain, sweat pouring down his ghastly pale face. She held him and tears began to well out of her eyes. "What's wrong, my brother? Do you have a stomach pain?"

"I am all right," So Ho said breathlessly.

"What is it? Do you want to go to the washroom?"

"Ask your friend to help me."

"I'll help you," Longevity said.

"Make my bed, Mai Mai," So Ho said. "I'll rest a little when I come back."

Mai Mai opened her brother's bedding while Longevity tried to help So Ho to the washroom. So Ho could hardly walk. Longevity tried to carry him, but his strength failed and they tumbled. Before they crashed into the railing, two strong hands grabbed them.

It was Mr. Carnahan. Mr. Quon, the scholarly Chinese, was with him. "Let somebody else help this sick man," Carnahan said. "This one is only a boy."

Old Wong, the butcher, eagerly squatted down. "I'll carry him," he said. He carried So Ho in the same manner he used to carry meat, hurrying away with one hand holding the load on his back and the other hand swinging.

Mai Mai watched them until they had disappeared into the hallway, her heart wringing with worry. As she knelt down to make her brother's bed, she saw two black shiny boots planted in front of her. She looked up and saw Mr. Carnahan staring down at her. "What's wrong with your brother?" Carnahan asked.

Mr. Quon translated the question.

"Stomach ache," Mai Mai said.

"What did he eat?"

"Same thing everybody else ate."

"Are you sure? Didn't he eat any of your own food that you've smuggled aboard?"

"No."

"Quon, tell them to throw all their stinky preserved food overboard. It's going to poison them all. We can't afford to have sick men."

Mr. Quon translated the order. A few men tossed their tins and cans into the ocean. Carnahan poked So Ho's belongings with a foot to see if he had any preserved food hidden in them, then he examined Mai Mai's luggage in the same manner. Mai Mai, still kneeling, stared at the busy boot and controlled a strong desire to grab it and bite the ankle.

"Listen, boy," he said to Mai Mai, "watch your

food. Don't you get sick too. And wash your face once in a while."

Mai Mai felt hurt. One day she would show the big foreigner how she really looked, in woman's dress; she wanted to make his eyes and mouth pop open in surprise.

So Ho did not come back from the washroom. Old Wong came back and hurried to the stern to wash. Mai Mai rushed to him but he told her not to come near him until he had thoroughly cleaned himself.

"What happened to my brother?" Mai Mai cried, almost forgetting that she was supposed to be a boy.

"He spat some blood," Old Wong said. "Nothing serious. The ship doctor is taking care of him now. Everybody has spat blood one time or another. I did three years ago; since then I have never felt better."

While Mai Mai was keeping a vigil, unable to eat or sleep, Four-eyed Dog volunteered to investigate So Ho's sickness. He came and went, busily passing out information he had gathered from Ah Hing and Mr. Quon. He finally reported that So Ho had been taken to the sickroom where the foreign doctor was going to cut him up, as the foreigners believed it was some invisible animals that had been causing So Ho's illness. "I say it is the evil spirits," he added, and quickly took out his pill box and swallowed another Snake Heart pill.

5

The next day most of the men were sick. Mai Mai sat beside her brother's well-made bed and stared at the hallway, waiting. Longevity had been sick earlier but then quickly adjusted to the rough sea and ate his beans, thick soup and bread with appetite. In fact, he began to like the rocking motion of the ship, and the deck was no harder than his bed at home.

Ta Ming, Old Wong, and a few other young men were the only ones who slept well. Four-eyed Dog slept with a musical band in his throat. The noise he produced had caused some complaints. When he woke up he was quiet, unable to eat anything but salted eggs and preserved beancake. He said he had brought some salted fish and would like to fry a piece or two to whet his appetite for the foreign food. The announcement horrified some of the law-abiding villagers, who warned Four-eyed Dog that the smell would bring the foreigners down like bloodhounds. "No cooking," Ta Ming said firmly, pointing a finger at Four-eyed Dog's large Adam's apple. "You don't want to get us all in trouble, do you?"

"Throw your stinky salted fish into the ocean," a man with a slit upper lip shouted. "We have all thrown ours away!"

"Don't say that, Split-lip Lee," Four-eyed Dog said. "You have thrown away your empty cans. Do you want me to search you?"

Split-lip Lee wanted to argue, but he thought better of it and kept quiet.

"I have lost my appetite," Four-eyed Dog moaned. "I feel weak. What am I going to do?"

"Talk less," Ta Ming advised.

"And think more, Four-eyed Dog," Old Wong added.

"Think of what?"

"Salted fish."

Four-eyed Dog swallowed a few times hungrily, his Adam's apple bobbing. "Ai, Old Wong," he said painfully, "why must you remind me of it? And please don't call me Four-eyed Dog on a foreign ship. Do you want me to lose my face and dignity in the eyes of the foreigners? I have a proper name."

"What is it?" Old Wong asked, winking.

"The surname is Chow."

"All right," Old Wong said with another wink. "From now on I'll call you Mr. Chow."

A mountainous wave hit the side of the ship with a tremendous roar. Four-eyed Dog's face whitened. A few men staggered toward the stern. Everybody was quiet for a moment. "Mr. Chow," Old Wong called. "*Wei*, Mr. Chow."

Four-eyed Dog did not respond. Old Wong called him a few more times, winking. Four-eyed Dog still did not recognize his new name. "*Wei*, Four-eyed Dog," Old Wong shouted.

"What? What?" Four-eyed Dog said, turning quickly.

That brought some laughter. After that Four-eyed Dog did not fuss over his name any more.

Mai Mai did not dislike Four-eyed Dog. She sometimes enjoyed listening to him talk and watching his Adam's apple. But each time she managed to keep far enough away from his spraying saliva. As she watched him she wished he had some information about her brother.

In the afternoon the sea was calmer, the sun began to shine between the low, heavy, dark clouds. Four-eyed Dog, who had eaten two salted eggs secretly, became active again. He came and went, talking and spraying saliva. Before meal time he brought news of importance. The foreign doctor had finally removed the invisible animals from So Ho's stomach and sewed him up again. Mai Mai almost jumped up and down and hugged him for the information.

To her disappointment Four-eyed Dog did not elaborate. He went on and talked about other things: the captain of the ship was an old foreign devil with a big black beard and a water-buffalo horn for a nose, who lived like a hermit in a little tower on the ship; the ship was one hundred twenty feet long and was named *Shooting Star;* it was armed with four cannons that had sunk many pirate ships.

He had also found out that Mr. Wilson was the number-one general on the ship, a Mr. Benson the number-two. There were five Chinese serving under them, headed by Ah Hing. "Do you know who Mr. Carnahan is?" he asked nobody in particular.

Nobody answered him.

"He is our employer," Four-eyed Dog went on significantly. "The owner of the gold mine in the foreign land where we are all going to become rich."

"Wei, Four-eyed Dog," Old Wong said, "I also have some exciting news to report. Do you know where the sun rises every morning? The east."

A few men laughed. Four-eyed Dog ignored the laughter and went on, "Do you know who that Chinese scholar is? Mr. Quon. He is Mr. Carnahan's partner, the first Chinese to settle down in a far, faraway foreign land. He limps a little. Do you know why?"

His listeners sat up and listened; they were interested. Four-eyed Dog enjoyed the attention. "So you all want to know why, eh? I'll tell you next time."

A few people grumbled.

"Wei, Four-eyed Dog," a man called Cat-fish Cheong asked, "where did you learn all these things?"

"From an important friend on this ship," Four-eyed

Dog said somewhat cockily. "Listen, if you will all chip in some money, I can ask this important man to sneak some salted fish into the mud-tasting foreign food tomorrow and we can all eat it with a good appetite. . . ."

"When will my brother come back?" Mai Mai asked, unable to wait any longer.

"Maybe in a day or two," he said knowingly. "He needs special care. His belly was just sewn up." Then he turned to the others again. *"Wei,* brothers, how about it? I have two salted fish wrapped in oil paper. Cost me five dollars each in the city of Canton. . . ."

"Did you see my brother?" Mai Mai asked.

"Sure I saw him. He is up and walking, his belly all sewed up, the invisible animals gone. Evil spirits. Nothing but plain evil spirits. A Taoist priest could have driven them away without having to resort to cutting. He will be back soon, Straw Sandal. Go wash your face. Now, about my salted fish—"

He was interrupted by the arrival of Mr. Carnahan, Mr. Wilson, and Mr. Quon. Everybody became quiet, holding his breath. Mr. Carnahan stared at the Chinese for a moment, his face expressionless. The air was tense. Finally Mr. Carnahan spoke. He solemnly announced the death of So Ho. He was sorry, and had requested the captain of the ship to accord So Ho the traditional burial at sea. Those who wished to attend the ceremony could follow him.

The blow was so sudden that for a moment Mai Mai did not feel the pain. When the pain came she steadied herself by holding onto the rail. She knew that she must not cry. She kept telling herself that death was only a happy occasion, a reunion of all ancestors in the other world where she, too, would eventually go.

Leading the way Mr. Carnahan started for the bow. The men followed him. Mai Mai waited. "So Ho will be all right," she told herself. "He will be happy." Longevity came to her and tugged at her sleeve. She dried her tears. He looked more like her younger brother now, same size, same height, same pigtail. . . .

"Aren't you going, Straw Sandal?" he asked.

"Yes, I'm going," she said.

At the bow the ceremony was just starting. So Ho's body, wrapped in a white sheet and placed on a board, was carried to the railing by two seamen. Unable to control herself at the sight of her brother's body, Mai Mai rushed forward to touch it, but was held back by Mr. Wilson. "All right, that's close enough," he said. "Go!"

The two seamen tipped the board and So Ho's body slipped into the sea, making a faint splash as it hit the water. Another seaman, standing nearby with a bugle, played a short note as Mr. Wilson and all the other seamen saluted in the direction of the bow.

Mai Mai quickly covered her face with her hands. "I mustn't cry like a woman," she told herself, pressing her eyes with her fingers so hard that they began to hurt. "I mustn't cry, I mustn't cry! So Ho will be happy. He is only making a trip to the other world to have a happy reunion with the ancestors."

Suddenly there was an angry murmur among the villagers.

"All right, go back," Mr. Carnahan said. "It is a

45

ceremony of high honor, worthy of the dead. I don't want to hear any complaints!"

Mai Mai couldn't make out what was wrong. The villagers started back for the stern quickly. Longevity followed his father, who looked ghastly pale. Mai Mai looked from one face to another, wondering why everybody was so angry. The silence was ominous.

After Mr. Carnahan, Mr. Wilson, and Mr. Quon had gone upstairs, Ta Ming stepped on somebody's crate that had served as a table, raised a hand and spoke, his voice quivering with anger. "How many of you saw So Ho kick?"

"I saw it," Four-eyed Dog shouted.

Everybody began to shout. All had seen it; they had seen one of So Ho's feet pull up in a short jerky motion under the white sheet when he was being slipped into the sea.

"He kicked!" Four-eyed Dog was shouting louder than everybody else. "He was trying to tell us he wasn't dead!" Now the angry voices almost drowned the roaring sea.

"The foreigners have thrown a man into the sea alive to save food!" one shouted. "It is murder!"

"The dead will never join his ancestors now!" another yelled.

"He will be a wandering ghost in the sea!"

"It is bad enough to go to a foreign land like this! Just think, not to be buried in one's ancestral burial grounds after he dies!"

"And what about his brother? Who is going to take care of him? He is only a boy. . . ."

"What did So Ho do in his life to deserve such a fate?"

"It is murder!"

"Murder!"

"Down with the foreigners!"

Ta Ming raised a hand and quieted everybody. "Listen, brothers," he said, "shouting will not solve problems. We shall delegate two older men to see the foreigners and demand an explanation of So Ho's death and a fair compensation for So Ho's family."

"You can read and write, you go!" Split-lip Lee shouted.

"Mr. Ling is a schoolteacher!"

Mr. Ling coughed and said he didn't feel well. Someone suggested that Old Wong could read and write, and was older.

Old Wong stood up and said modestly that he knew only enough writing to keep an honest account of his meat business. But as for age, he had to admit that he was everybody's senior, except Mr. Ling's. If Mr. Ling was ill and there was no one else who was better educated, he would be happy to represent the group.

By unanimous vote Old Wong and Ta Ming were elected as the delegates.

While waiting for the delegates to return, the villagers sat on the deck tensely. A few expressed their fear of offending the foreigners, but most remained quietly angry. Longevity was busy trying to console Mai Mai. He kept rubbing her limp hands. Four-eyed Dog got up, took off his blue cotton blouse, wound his pigtail around his head and started shadowboxing, saying that everybody should limber up and be ready for action.

Mr. Ling did not want any trouble. He took out a string of beads which he rubbed with his thumb, murmuring a Buddhist prayer. Split-lip Lee produced a piece of old jade and rubbed on it, confiding to Longevity that the jade had the power to drive away evil spirits. Since Longevity was trying to console the dead man's brother, he gave Longevity the privilege of rubbing it a few times for luck.

Finally Mai Mai opened her eyes. She lay on the hard cold deck and stared at the cloudless sky dry-eyed and unfeeling. Longevity poured a cup of water from her gourd and tried to make her drink. She did not respond. He poured the water slowly between her lips, but most of it trickled out from the corners of her mouth.

"He is not dead, is he?" Split-lip Lee said, feeling Mai Mai's pulse.

"He is breathing," Longevity said.

Split-lip Lee rubbed Mai Mai's hand against his jade a few times. "Just for good luck. Such a soft hand. Poor boy. Probably did not do a stitch of work all his life. How is he going to take care of himself?"

The Chinese waited for almost an hour before the delegates returned. Old Wong looked dejected, his thick lower lip sticking way out, almost hiding his short chin. Ta Ming was grim, his jaw bones moving. Everybody stared at them, waiting tensely for them to speak. Ta Ming took a deep breath. "Brothers, the foreigners insisted that So Ho was dead when they buried him in the sea. They refuse to pay any compensation to his family. But we asked Mr. Quon to speak to the foreigners again. In case of death in the future, we want the body of the dead to be shipped back to China, so that the relatives of the dead can bury him in his ancestral burial grounds."

There was an immediate response. All the villagers began to talk at once.

"We want a guarantee!" one shouted.

"Yes, a guarantee!" another agreed. "Who wants to become a wandering ghost in a foreign land?"

"I wouldn't like to be one for all the gold in the world."

"If the foreigners don't guarantee that, I demand to be sent back!"

"May the Jade Emperor in heaven have mercy on So Ho's lost soul!"

"When we get paid we shall all donate something for his brother, his widow and children."

"He may even have old parents too, all eating grass roots and waiting for his return."

"Let us all go back! Who wants to die in a foreign land like a wild dog?"

"If I had known what the foreigners eat, I would not have come, gold or no gold!"

"I agree!" Four-eyed Dog shouted. "I demand the right to eat my own salted fish! Right now!"

Ta Ming raised a hand and quieted everybody. "Brothers," he said, "it is too early to talk about other demands. Let us wait calmly for Mr. Quon's report. He promised to bring us an early answer. Being a Chinese himself, he understands our feelings."

It did not take long for Mr. Quon to bring them the

answer. The foreigners had rejected the request and warned the villagers not to make a nuisance of themselves. Mr. Quon spoke impersonally, his face stern. The Chinese were stunned. Mr. Quon, after a sweeping glance at the hundred-odd angry faces, lifted up his silk gown and quickly limped upstairs.

There was a murmur, then some men began to shout again. Once more Ta Ming quieted everybody. He conducted a conference and discussed the next step. The majority favored Old Wong's suggestion that they all go upstairs and demand to be sent back home. They could eat any foreign food and sleep in ice or fire, but they could not permit themselves to be buried just anywhere in case of death. That was their only and absolute demand. Four-eyed Dog still wanted the privilege of frying his salted fish, but he was shouted down.

Led by Old Wong, the men marched toward the stairway. Before they reached it, six seamen, headed by Mr. Wilson, armed with pistols, rushed down and blocked the passageway. Mr. Wilson fired his pistol over the Chinese's heads and warned them not to come one step closer. The Chinese stood their ground defiantly. Mr. Wilson stepped forward and ordered the Chinese to go back to the stern, or else, he said, the officers would be forced to shoot them down.

The Chinese did not understand him. Some waved their fists and shouted defiance. A few advanced.

"All right, men, let them have it!" Mr. Wilson shouted. Just as the seamen raised their pistols ready to shoot, Mr. Quon, who had arrived with Mr. Carnahan, rushed forward and shouted "Stop!" in both English and Chinese.

The advancing Chinese halted. The seamen, who had raised their weapons, waited. "Listen," Mr. Carnahan said to the Chinese, "you have not come to get killed, and I have no use for a heap of corpses. I have considered your request and regard it as not unreasonable. The misunderstanding stemmed from our different customs and traditions. If to be buried in your ancestral grounds is that important to you, we shall not stand between you and your dead ancestors. After all, shipping a corpse back is not as expensive as a live man. So your wish is granted. Now go back and enjoy the trip. It is still a long way to the Land of the Golden Mountain."

After Mr. Quon translated, the Chinese nodded and grunted, expressing their satisfaction. Old Wong shouted that he wanted a written guarantee. A few others agreed with him, demanding the same. Faces became red again and another angry hubbub started.

Ta Ming made the demand formally through Mr. Quon. Mr. Carnahan glared. "All right," he said with a wave of his hand, "we shall give you a collective guarantee, to be duly signed and dated. Mr. Quon will write it in Chinese." He turned and went upstairs, followed by Mr. Quon, Mr. Wilson, and the armed seamen.

The villagers considered Mr. Carnahan's offer after some argument among themselves. Finally they decided to accept the collective guarantee. They elected Ta Ming to examine the contents and assigned Old Wong to lock the guarantee in his chest for safekeeping.

"Curse their ancestors!" Four-eyed Dog said after everybody had expressed his satisfaction. "I still can't fry my salted fish." He resumed his shadowboxing, repeating loudly that the troubles were not over and that everybody should still limber up for action.

Split-lip Lee, looking worried, dug out his jade piece and rubbed it some more. "Somebody has brought evil spirits to this ship," he said. "Rub it, Longevity."

Longevity did not have much confidence in the old jade, but he rubbed it a few times for luck, anyhow.

6

The sea was calm, the ship sailed smoothly and a few seagulls had once more appeared, circling around the stern. The coolies consumed the evening meal with good appetite, sucking in air and smacking their lips.

Mai Mai ate her dinner slowly, trying not to think of her brother. She avoided looking at his meager belongings, the sight of which made her throat swell. The urge to cry was so great that she had to bite her tongue to suppress it.

When the meal was over Longevity came and sat beside her. "I still have some watermelon seeds," he said, opening the parcel and offering it to Mai Mai. The handful of brownish melon seeds lying on the worn-out coarse wrapping paper reminded Mai Mai of her brother again. She quickly covered her face with both her hands and bit her tongue sharply. "What's the matter?" Longevity asked. "Do you have a headache?"

Mai Mai shook her head. "If you want to sneeze," Longevity advised, "take a deep breath and hold it. It will stop."

"I am all right now," Mai Mai said, forcing a smile.

"You have nothing to worry about, Straw Sandal. My father said he would take care of both of us."

"Thank him for me, Longevity, but I'm a big boy now. I can take care of myself."

"I can take care of myself too. But the foreigners won't let us. When we arrive in the gold mines we shall show them, Straw Sandal. I have more muscles and strength than a lot of older men. If anyone wants to bet me a package of roasted watermelon seeds that I can't beat Four-eyed Dog in a fight, or lift Mr. Ling up with one small finger, I'll double the bet. You are pretty strong too, Straw Sandal. And you are big for your age. If your voice changed a little, you could be a grown-up man."

"I am a grown-up man."

"When we go back to China, with our pockets full of gold, you can marry my cousin. She is my mother's niece; she is hard working and plump. When we have another famine, she will be the last one to become skinny. And plump women are fertile; she can give you a lot of sons."

"Thank you, Longevity. I certainly hope to meet her when I go back to China."

"She is thirteen now. In a year or two she will be ready for marriage. My mother married my father when she was fourteen. Are you fifteen?"

"Yes."

"My father married my mother when he was fifteen. If my mother had been plump like her niece, she could have given my father fifteen sons already."

"When did she die?"

"Last year. When she died she was all skin and bones. The famine killed her. When my father returns to China with a lot of gold, we are going to give her a big belated funeral, burn a large paper house, five paper servants and a chest of gold. Not real gold— gold made of golden paper. Ghosts cannot touch anything unless we burn it first. Do you want to know a secret?"

"Yes."

Longevity cast a glance over his shoulder, lowered his voice and confided, "Mr. Ling has brought a lot of paper money, the kind you burn at a grave for your ancestors. If you want to burn some for your brother, I can steal some for you."

"No, Longevity. My brother wouldn't like to have anyone steal for him."

"Mr. Ling is very stingy. We know him. He wouldn't give anything to anybody, unless you pay for it. Do you have any real money?"

"No."

"Me neither. So you see? The only way to get it is to borrow it when he is asleep. We can pay him for it when my father has made some money from the foreigners. Why are you crying?"

"I accidentally bit my tongue. I am all right, Longevity."

Mai Mai looked away, biting her tongue hard to keep the lump in her throat from swelling again. She felt that her younger brother, who had died a year earlier, had suddenly come back to life and was now sitting beside her trying to soothe her and comfort her. Had So Ho known that he was going to die? Was that why he had urged her to befriend Longevity?

Then she saw the pair of shining boots again. Slowly she lifted her eyes. She knew who it was and she was afraid of him. In fact, she had developed a fear of all foreigners since So Ho's death. When she saw Mr. Quon standing behind the foreigner, she felt better.

"Hardly touched your food, eh?" Mr. Carnahan said. "Well, I don't blame you. Don't worry, boy, we'll take care of you, whether you are strong enough to work in the mines or not."

As soon as Mr. Quon finished translating, Mr. Carnahan went on, "But you must eat, boy. You've survived the famine in China. It would be a joke if you died of starvation on a ship loaded with food. Quon, ask him if he wants to eat with us."

Mr. Quon asked. Mai Mai shook her head.

"Well, bring him upstairs anyway when the next meal is served," Carnahan said. "I would lose my appetite too if I were fed this greasy stuff every day."

"Listen, Straw Sandal," Mr. Quon said sternly, "Mr. Carnahan wants you to eat with him and the captain. Don't be so foolish as to shake your head again.

You can't afford to miss a good meal, being so pale and skinny. I'll come and take you upstairs before the next meal."

After Mr. Carnahan and Mr. Quon had left, a serious discussion started among the Chinese on the subject of whether or not Straw Sandal should accept the invitation. There were pros and cons, and quite a few bet on the outcome.

"I say," Four-eyed Dog said, "it's up to Straw Sandal to make up his own mind. I certainly approve of his going if he can slip a ham or a chicken under his blouse every meal. We can all have a taste of what the foreigners eat upstairs."

Mai Mai did not express her opinion; she just sat quietly staring into space. When Mr. Quon came to take her upstairs the air became more tense. The men almost held their breath waiting to see what she would do.

Four-eyed Dog nudged Old Wong and whispered, "Want to bet? Last chance!" Old Wong ignored him, but watched Mai Mai tensely.

After a glance at Longevity, Mai Mai stood up and followed Mr. Quon upstairs. Many sighed with relief. A few stretched out their hands to others to collect their winnings.

In the dining room upstairs Mai Mai felt a little nervous. At the round table four foreigners had already started on their soup. Mr. Carnahan was sitting at the table facing the entrance. On his right was Mr. Wilson, on his left was a small man with a red beard and a hooked nose. Mr. Benson, the man who had accused her of stealing, was sitting with his back toward the door. Waiting on the table was a Chinese seaman in a white uniform. The darkish panelled room was small, furnished with heavy hardwood chairs.

"Sit down, boy," Mr. Carnahan said, pointing to one of the two empty chairs opposite him. "Quon, introduce him to the captain."

As Mr. Quon introduced them, the man with the red beard and hooked nose peered at Mai Mai with narrowed eyes and nodded.

"The poor boy lost his brother," Mr. Carnahan said. "Lost his appetite too." He turned to Mai Mai and added, "Try the soup, boy. See if you like this food better."

Mai Mai liked the thick pea soup smelling of smoked ham. She ate it quietly and stole an occasional glance at the captain. Four-eyed Dog had said that the captain had a buffalo horn for a nose. It was indeed shaped like a horn. She wondered if it was just as hard. She felt a strong desire to pinch it.

"Quon," the captain said, "you Chinamen eat soup with a lot of noise as an established etiquette. If this boy wants to eat like a Chinaman, tell him to go ahead. We don't mind."

Mr. Quon told her. Mai Mai smacked her lips.

"Do you want a pair of chopsticks, boy?" Carnahan asked. Without waiting for Mr. Quon to translate, he ordered the seaman to bring a pair of chopsticks to the table.

"How can a Chinaman pick up food with two sticks? That I'll never know," the captain said with a laugh.

"Captain," Carnahan said, "if the boy likes the food, I want him to eat with us for the rest of the journey. Hope you have no objection."

"It's against the ship's rules."

"You are the skipper of the ship. You can change the rules."

"It's highly irregular."

"It's highly irregular to let a boatswain operate on a sick man."

"The boatswain had two years of medical training. He treats everybody on this ship." The captain turned to the first mate and asked, "He treated you too, didn't he, Mr. Wilson?"

"Yes, sir. He pulled one of my teeth."

"He may be able to pull a tooth," Carnahan said, "but he is hardly qualified to diagnose a man's illness, and then treat him by simply taking his appendix out. For all I know the sick man might have been suffering an attack of malaria, or acute indigestion. I would say food poison—"

"Mr. Carnahan," the captain interrupted, "those Chinamen die like flies. The famine had killed thousands of them."

"That's no reason why . . ." Carnahan stopped. He decided not to continue the subject. He stuffed a piece of meat into his mouth and chewed it busily.

"Mr. Quon," the captain said, "tell this boy we are all very sorry about his brother's death. Ask him if he likes the sea. If he does, I may try him out as a cabin boy."

"Now, Captain," Carnahan cut in, "if you think you

can make a seaman out of him, there is no reason why I can't make a miner out of him."

"He is only a boy," the captain said. "There are things a boy can do on a ship."

"There are things that a boy can do in a mining camp, too. Quon, tell the boy if he likes California, he can work on less strenuous jobs until he is big enough to dig. If he prefers going back to China, that can be arranged too."

Mr. Quon translated. Mai Mai didn't know what to do. She had no desire to go back to Heavenly Tranquillity. Yet the foreign land was so far, far away. Suddenly a terrible loneliness gnawed at her. She wished she were a man.

"What's your name, boy?" the captain asked.

"Straw Sandal."

"How do you like the food, Straw Sandal?"

Mai Mai liked the smoked pork. She had already slipped a piece of it into her pocket for Longevity. She liked the other things too. The baked potato smelled almost like rice; the warm bread with the crispy crust tasted so different from the sour bread she had eaten downstairs. The only thing that she didn't care for too much was the black juice called coffee; it tasted like Chinese herb medicine, something she could never swallow without making a face.

"Well, boy," Mr. Carnahan said, "the captain offered you a job. Do you want to work on this ship or would you rather go to California?"

Mai Mai looked between the captain and Mr. Carnahan, then glanced at Mr. Wilson and Mr. Benson, who grinned at her. They all looked very friendly. But where was the doctor who had treated her brother? She asked.

"He is eating in his cabin," the captain said.

"He killed my brother."

"Boy, don't make accusations like that!" the captain said sharply. "Your brother died of serious illness. Mr. Nicholson tried to save him but it was too late."

Mai Mai hated this Mr. Nicholson. She had yet to convince herself that death was a happy occasion, a re-union of all ancestors. But if her brother was really happy after death, he certainly wouldn't want her to argue with the foreigners now. "I don't blame anybody for my brother's death," she said. "It is the will of the Jade Emperor in heaven."

After Mr. Quon translated, the captain said with a loud laugh, "Well, here's a heathen boy who talks like a Christian. Young man, you still have a choice of having an easy life on this ship or going to rough it in Califor-nia. You make up your own mind."

"I am going to California," Mai Mai said.

The captain peered at her, somewhat surprised. Mr. Carnahan smiled. Mai Mai slipped a potato into her pocket, took a sip of her coffee and tried not to make a face. The potato felt warm and heavy in her pocket. "Longevity will love it," she thought, and stuffed a big-ger one into her other pocket when nobody was look-ing.

"Well, Captain," Carnahan said, "how about it? Shall we let the boy eat upstairs for the rest of the jour-ney?"

"It's highly irregular."

"All right." Carnahan forked a large piece of

smoked pork onto Mai Mai's plate. "Boy, this is your last meal upstairs. Eat as much as you can. If you can't eat it, take it."

"Mr. Carnahan," the captain said, "if it will make you happy, I'll allow the boy to come and eat the leftovers every day."

Carnahan rose. "Quon, tell the boy of the captain's invitation. Tell him it's a rotten honor but if I were he I wouldn't decline it. It's a pleasure eating all by yourself —and he won't have to observe any table manners."

7

 Mai Mai did not decline the captain's invitation.
She enjoyed the foreign food, but she still longed for a
good Chinese chicken or pork dish cooked in lard and
spiced with star anise seeds or dried mushrooms. Every
day she brought leftovers to Longevity, who ate them
secretly. As a result Longevity became a moon-faced
and rosy-cheeked boy who often sat on the deck looking
groggy. This puzzled his father considerably.

The trip from China to San Francisco lasted two
months and five days. Before the *Shooting Star* entered

San Francisco Bay, Mr. Carnahan shaved his beard. Mai Mai almost did not recognize him. He looked young and handsome, with a strong jaw and excellent sparkling teeth, which had been buried in his thick mustache before.

The last day on the ship was an occasion. The Chinese had the best dinner of the trip—ham and potato. They had had so much stew that the solid food became a treat. Chopstick Lew ate it ravenously in spite of a toothache. Mr. Ling took a few secret swigs from a little jar that everybody believed was rice wine. For the first time, Four-eyed Dog did not talk much, claiming that one must concentrate while eating ham, or the smoke flavor would escape from the mouth.

Mai Mai went upstairs a little earlier than usual. She was permitted to wait in a corner while the officers ate. The captain ordered champagne and toasted everybody. Mr. Carnahan delivered a speech. By going upstairs every day Mai Mai had learned some English. She understood half of what Mr. Carnahan said.

In his brief speech Mr. Carnahan expressed his gratitude to the captain for the speedy and safe journey; his only regret was that the Chinese had not gained any weight in spite of the daily servings of excellent rotten beans and sour bread. However, he added, there were a few compensations. For one thing, the foreign devils' food made the journey seem so long and so dull to the Chinese that they had all become more anxious to go to the mines to dig gold for him. Moreover, the men's poor appetites actually saved money for him, as he had originally planned to pay freight on every ounce of weight the Chinese might have gained during the trip. Now, nothing gained and nothing more to pay. Paying always pained him. So all in all the trip was a success, and he would like to return the captain's toast. He stood up and downed his champagne. The captain downed his, wetting the tip of his hooked nose in the process. Mai Mai watched him and controlled an urge to giggle.

It was a foggy morning when the *Shooting Star* edged its way through the Golden Gate and into San Francisco Bay. The Chinese lined the railings and viewed, with awe and expectation, the Land of the Golden Mountain.

The journey had indeed been monotonous. They were all anxious to reach their destination, and the prospect of cooking their own food again was exciting.

They had learned a great deal about the foreign land. Some had even picked up a few words of English. But nobody had learned as much as Mai Mai and Longevity, who had studied the foreign talk from the foreign seamen. Longevity swore a lot but the foreign tongue still sounded very impressive. Ta Ming was proud of him.

Four-eyed Dog had completely forgotten his salted fish; he had long since eaten it raw. His latest information was that the foreign land was sparsely populated by two kinds of people, the hairy white ones and the crimson-colored ones who went around stark naked. These two peoples warred against each other so often that Ah Hing, the ship's chef, brought a special warning to his fellow-countrymen: Never stand between a white man and a crimson-colored man, for they might start shooting at each other on sight, one with a gun and the other with a poisonous arrow.

According to Ah Hing, the crimson-colored men were not too friendly to outsiders. They ate raw meat, their favorite dish being the front part of a white man's head. So far there had been no stories about a Chinese being eaten, but it was wise to avoid them and be sure to show one's pigtail when confronting one.

Longevity was also full of information. He knew how much Mr. Carnahan was going to pay the Chinese —10 percent of the gold the Chinese mined. He told Mai Mai not to worry. Ten percent would make everyone rich. According to Four-eyed Dog, the foreign land was so rich with gold that if a man picked up a rock and hit a wild dog with it, nine times out of ten he would have tossed away a gold nugget.

With some misgivings Mai Mai stared at the strange land while the *Shooting Star* cast anchor. The fog was lifting. The bay was crowded with sailing ships and the land was green and hilly.

Mr. Carnahan, wearing a brand new red shirt and his usual shiny boots, was busy giving directions. He ordered the Chinese to be rowed ashore at East Bay in little boats manned by the crew of the *Shooting Star*. He leaped up and down from the ship to a boat and from the boat to the dock with such agility that Mai Mai thought he must have been a monkey in his previous life.

Mr. Quon was the cautious type; he never took his foot off a boat until he had set his other foot on solid ground.

The little town in East Bay, a motley jumble of tents and wooden buildings backed by miles of sand dunes, was somewhat unsightly. Mr. Carnahan and Mr. Quon herded the Chinese along a muddy street to a crowded marketplace where half a dozen mule carts were waiting. Mai Mai and Longevity walked side by side, following Ta Ming, each carrying his own luggage in a bundle tied on his back. Mr. Quon gave strict instructions in Cantonese that everybody must stay together.

"That's right," Four-eyed Dog agreed loudly. "Let nobody saunter off, not even a few feet from the next man, lest he run into a crimson-colored man."

"Politeness wards off danger," Mr. Ling commented. "A deep bow will turn an enemy into a friend."

"I'm not going to bow to anyone, white or crimson-colored," Split-lip Lee retorted. "All I care about is reaching the mines quickly and starting to dig for gold."

"I won't dig until I have cooked myself a good Chinese dinner," Catfish Cheong said.

Mai Mai was busy looking and studying the foreign land with the strange-looking people who in turn studied her and the other Chinese curiously. Most men in the marketplace wore red shirts like Mr. Carnahan's, but quite a few were gaudily dressed in satin coats and colorful vests with gold watch chains hanging across them. There were others whose clothes were dirty and sloppy. The dirty ones all wore beards, chewed tobacco, and squirted brown juice from their mouths.

"Are they spitting blood?" Longevity asked.

"They don't look sick," Mai Mai said. "Ignore them, Longevity. They are all staring at us."

While the mule carts were being loaded with large

sacks of provisions, Mr. Carnahan mounted an energetic white horse, gave Mr. Quon the final instructions, spurred the horse and rode away. When the carts were all loaded, Mr. Quon told the coolies to follow them. He himself climbed on the last cart and sat beside the driver. "Not too far to walk," he told the Chinese. "Then we shall take a boat up the Sacramento River."

The dusty winding trail was not too different from those in China. There were green hills covered with pines and cypress. For a while Mai Mai kept her eyes on the trail looking for gold. Longevity picked up a few rocks and examined them. He was disappointed that they were not gold nuggets.

"Longevity," Ta Ming said, "every man has a story. When a second man tells the first man's story, he is likely to put soy sauce in it to make it more tasty. Don't ever believe what Four-eyed Dog tells you. He always adds legs to a snake." He scanned the scenery and sighed, "Look at this land. There is more than gold in this soil."

Mai Mai looked at the scenery and cast an occasional glance at Ta Ming. His profile looked handsomer than ever to her. She felt faintly happy and was glad that she had come.

They walked quietly for a while. When they reached a little town, the sun had fallen behind the hills. "This is Benicia," Mr. Quon said. "We shall stay here for the night."

They found a wooded area and the three mule drivers pitched a tent. Two went inside to sleep and one guarded the mules, gun in hand.

The Chinese rested under the oak trees assigned by

Mr. Quon, who gave strict orders that nobody was to wander away from the area. At daybreak, they were to proceed farther inland by boat.

Mai Mai lay on her back beside Longevity. She could feel the cool damp soil under her blanket. Above, the oak tree extended like an enormous umbrella. A small distant moon shone among the leaves, which rustled slightly in the breeze. Insects chirped noisily. Mai Mai listened to them, and was surprised that they sounded exactly like those singing in the summer nights at her village. The country smelled the same, too; even the foreign moon looked just like the one in China. She felt like talking, but Longevity was asleep.

Besides the singing of insects, a coyote howled in the distance. A few men talked; others began to snore. Four-eyed Dog had become strangely quiet. Old Wong asked him what had sewn his mouth up. Four-eyed Dog said tersely that he was thinking of gold and wished not to be disturbed.

When Mai Mai was awakened by a man's groaning she had no idea what time it was. The moon had moved into an open space between the branches of the oak tree and shone brightly in the starlit sky. She stared at the moon and listened to the groaning, wondering who was ill. She noticed that Ta Ming and the others around her all tossed and turned under their covers, disturbed by the sick man.

Finally a few men got up to find out what had happened. It turned out that two men were ill. Chopstick Lew, who groaned, was suffering from a nameless pain. The other sick man was a quiet farmer named Toy Sing, who had been feverish and twisting in silence. Ta

Ming, who knew some herb medicine, was attending him. He examined Toy's pulse and tongue and consulted with Old Wong, who diagnosed the sickness as "the grinding disease of the intestine." Ta Ming agreed with him and asked if anyone had brought any pain relievers such as Eight Diagram Pills or Gold Rat Pills. Five men had them and they all eagerly dug out their pill boxes to help.

Having ministered the pain reliever and given the sick men some water, Ta Ming went to hunt for roots of Dog Tail Weed, an herb good for many sicknesses and nameless pains. Hardly had he walked ten feet than a shot tore through the air. Mai Mai saw Ta Ming's shadow fall heavily to the ground. She muffled a cry. Longevity leaped up and dashed to his father. Almost immediately there was another ringing shot and a bullet struck the dirt, narrowly missing Longevity. "Halt!" somebody shouted.

"Don't move!" another shouted in Cantonese. "Lie down!"

Mai Mai recognized Ta Ming's voice. Longevity obeyed quickly. Nobody was hurt. Mai Mai sighed with relief. She heard a few men swear and ask what was going on. Then she saw the shadows of two men hurry to Longevity. She strained her eyes and found that one was the guard and the other Mr. Quon. Beyond them two other men were guarding Ta Ming. One was aiming his gun at him.

Mai Mai moved closer and heard Mr. Quon ask both Ta Ming and Longevity what they were doing. It was not until after a long explanation from Ta Ming that Mr. Quon believed it was all a mistake. The mule drivers had thought that Ta Ming intended to steal their mules and that Longevity had tried to escape.

"All right," Mr. Quon said to Ta Ming and Longevity, "go back to sleep. As for the sick, we shall attend to them in the riverboat. It is lucky that the mule drivers did not kill you two. Otherwise I would have two sick men and two corpses on my hands. You cannot blame them for shooting. In this country, horse thieves are everywhere. Remember, don't ever touch a man's horse. You can steal his wife but never touch his horse. That's the unwritten law in this foreign land."

"Hey," the guard with the shotgun said to Mr. Quon, pointing at Chopstick Lew, tell him to stop that infernal groaning."

"He is ill," Mr. Quon said. "Groaning relieves pain —Chinese way."

"Your Chinese way gives me a pain in the neck."

"It keeps the horse thieves away too," Mr. Quon explained patiently.

The guard thought for a moment. "Groaning relieves pain, eh? I'll try that next time a mule kicks me."

He spat some brown juice and returned to the tent, followed by the other two men. Mr. Quon took out his large gold watch, narrowed his eyes and looked at it closely. "Two more hours before we start up river," he told the villagers. "Try to sleep some more."

After Mr. Quon had returned to his tent, everybody lay down again. Mai Mai stared at the moon, unable to sleep. Four-eyed Dog became talkative. He asked if anybody wanted to know who Mr. Quon really was. Though nobody answered him, he told the story about Mr. Quon anyway, to nobody in particular.

He said that Mr. Quon was once a famous gambler who lost his leg because a rival gambler planted a rattlesnake in his bed. The snake bit his ankle. Mr. Quon cut his pigtail and tied his leg with it to prevent the poison from going up his body. Then he cut the leg off with a pair of scissors. According to Ah Hing, Mr. Quon still had that pair of scissors, soaked in a jar of vinegar. He kept it as a souvenir and reminder, and slept beside it. "Do you know what happened to the other gambler?" he asked.

He paused for dramatic effect. His listeners pretended that they were not interested. He went on, "Mr. Quon avenged himself by sending the other gambler a copy of *The Plum Flower in a Golden Vase*—a dirty book full of details. The other gambler read it hungrily, wetting his fingers to turn the pages. In ten minutes he died—killed by the poison Mr. Quon had smeared on the corners of every page."

Mai Mai stared at the sky and thought of Mr. Quon. She wondered how much soy sauce Four-eyed Dog had added to this story. Too bad it was told by Four-eyed Dog. She could have believed it one hundred percent if it had been told by someone else. But she hoped the story was true. If Four-eyed Dog had added legs to a snake, as Ta Ming had put it, she wanted it that way—it was so odd and exciting.

She heard Longevity turn restlessly. "You can't sleep either, Longevity?" she whispered.

"I'm not sleepy," Longevity said.

"The moon is too bright. It makes me think of home. Wonder what my younger brother is doing now."

"I wonder who Mr. Quon is," Longevity said.

"Four-eyed Dog says he is a gambler."

"I don't believe him. *Wei*, Straw Sandal, do you know what *The Plum Flower in a Golden Vase* is?"

"It's a forbidden book."

"Why?"

"You are too young to know these things, Longevity. Go to sleep."

"Can you read, Straw Sandal?"

"Yes."

"I can't."

"Good," Mai Mai said. "So nobody can poison you by sending you a book to read. Go to sleep now, Longevity."

Both closed their eyes and tried to sleep.

8

The Sacramento River did not look too different from the Pearl River in China. Both were muddy and wide. The only difference was that the foreign river did not have sampans, and the trees on the banks were thicker and taller.

Before sunrise Mr. Carnahan was already on the river giving directions, pointing and shouting orders. The steamboat, old and rickety, sat on the water like a fat duck with a big tail.

Toy Sing had to be carried aboard. Chopstick Lew was still groaning loudly. Mr. Carnahan thought his case was serious, but Mr. Quon reminded him that the louder a Chinese sick man groaned the less sick he became. It was true in Chopstick Lew's case. Everybody ignored him and he went aboard under his own steam, staggering a little, but not enough to fall off the gangplank.

Shortly before the boat sailed, Four-eyed Dog learned that the boat was thirty-five feet long, that it had been leased by Mr. Carnahan and was piloted by Mr. Carnahan's other two partners, Mr. King and Mr. Gordon.

Mai Mai had seen the two men, who had been hurrying up and down, shouting and loading the ship. Both were lanky and wore red shirts. Four-eyed Dog significantly pointed out that the taller one with the livid scar running across his right cheek was Mr. King. "Do you know who he is? Well, I'll tell you next time."

When the ship sailed it gave such a sharp whistle that Longevity jumped. The big wheel in the back turned, churning the water and muddying it. Wild ducks in the nearby reeds flew away in fright, squawking noisily.

Mai Mai had never seen a steamboat before. She was fascinated by the noise and the vibration. Both she and Longevity watched the big wheel wide-eyed, gaping in awe.

"It is rowed by a giant," Four-eyed Dog said.

"Where?" Longevity asked, looking to his right and left.

"He is lying down under the deck. See that tall

pipe? He breathes through it. That smoke is his breath."

"I don't believe you."

"As you please."

Mr. Quon, who looked cheerful, went around talking to the villagers. He said that the *Sea Gull* was the only steamboat in California, the fastest boat on the Sacramento River. Ordinarily a miner would take one of those small bluff-nosed sailboats to the river from San Francisco Bay, but the journey would take a day longer. This way they would get to the mines ahead of one thousand other men. Yes, one thousand men, Mr. Quon said emphatically. That was how many prospectors were pouring into the Mother Lode Country every day to find gold.

"This is the big gold rush," he pointed out. "The harder a man works the faster he will be rich. In the mines nobody can afford to be lazy, for gold in the mines is like rice in a tub that is not bottomless."

The coolies listened with great interest; some rubbed their hands together eagerly. "Looks like we have no time to cook a Chinese dinner," Old Wong said.

"When I am rich," Catfish Cheong said, "I'll do nothing but eat. And take a wife who will do nothing but cook. Now is no time to think of food." He tightened his belt with a nod of finality.

The boat gained speed, vibrating less now. The sun had risen and dispelled the morning chill. Longevity was busy looking between the beautiful spray that dashed away from the bow. He was afraid he would miss something.

For a long time the boat sailed on the wide, calm

river lined with tall weeds. Straight ahead rose the distant blue mountains. Mai Mai had never seen so many wild ducks and geese and other nameless black birds. Startled by the steamboat, the birds soared into the air with a roar, some quacking, some screaming.

Chopstick Lew had stopped groaning. Toy Sing, pale and dried-up, lay on the deck with his sunken eyes closed. Mr. Carnahan, his black boots dusty, never stopped rushing around giving instructions. He finally came to the sick men, inspected them with a heavy scowl, and went away looking grim. Mr. Quon limped after him, talking. Both disappeared into a cabin that had glass widows and red curtains.

Four-eyed Dog worked himself to a high pitch of enthusiasm over what he was going to see and do. "With the first gold I make I'm going to buy a gun," he said, "and shoot those ducks. I have three hundred different ways to cook a duck. But I like the beggar's way the best."

Then he went on to explain how a beggar prepared his duck. "First, catch the duck, of course. Then build a fire, naturally. Pack the duck in mud; make a mud ball out of it. Throw the ball into the fire and let it bake. After two hours crack the mud ball open and there you are, the cooked duck, fragrant and delicious, with all the feathers pulled off by the dried mud, clean as a baby after a bath."

Four-eyed Dog gesticulated and sprayed saliva as he described the taste of the beggar's duck, his large Adam's apple jumping. Longevity kept swallowing, but he claimed loudly that he did not like duck, no matter how it was cooked. Four-eyed Dog enjoyed torturing the boy; he went on and described a few other ways to cook duck.

"Longevity," Ta Ming called. "Go ask Mr. Quon to come quickly."

Ta Ming and a few others were now squatting beside Toy. Longevity, absorbed by Four-eyed Dog's descriptions of food, looked reluctant to leave. "I'll go for you, Longevity," Mai Mai said.

She hurried to Ta Ming and asked what was wrong.

"Toy Sing is dead," Ta Ming said.

She had watched many relatives die; she had seen numerous corpses on the streets in Heavenly Tranquillity, but the tortured look of Toy was something new; it made her shiver.

She rapped on the cabin door. Mr. Carnahan opened it. "Yes?"

Mai Mai stammered out what had happened. She felt sick in the stomach.

"Quon," Carnahan said, "find out what this boy is babbling about."

Mr. Quon was sitting on a bunk puffing on a long bamboo pipe. On the small table in front of him was a large map with red circles on it. He translated what Mai Mai had said.

"So he kicked the bucket," Mr. Carnahan said with a frown. "These men drop like flies. By the time we reach the mines we'll have nothing but a bunch of corpses."

"Only two have died," Mr. Quon said calmly.

"Two! We haven't reached the mines yet!"

"I'd better go give them a kind word," Mr. Quon said, rising.

When Mai Mai started to follow Mr. Quon, Carnahan stopped her. 'Boy," he said in bad Cantonese, "you shoe shine?"

"Y—yes," Mai Mai said haltingly. She was a little surprised by Carnahan's tone of voice, which was no longer friendly.

"Shine my boots," Carnahan ordered, sitting down on the bunk and stretching his long legs.

On the bunk was a rag. Carnahan jerked a finger at it. Mai Mai hesitated. "Hop hop!" Carnahan said in English. "Nobody idles in this country. Here everybody works for a living. The sooner you know that the better."

Mai Mai picked up the rag and started working on Mr. Carnahan's black boots. She was a little unhappy about Carnahan's change of attitude. She glanced up resentfully. Carnahan was busy studying the map with the red circles on it. "When I'm no longer a coolie boy," she told herself, "I'll make this foreigner stare at me just like all the other men did on the street in Heavenly Tranquillity. I'll show him."

Swallowing her pride she shined Carnahan's boots vigorously. When she finished Carnahan lowered his map and peeked at his boots. "Hm, not bad. Do you cook?"

"Yes."

"Boy, you've got yourself a job. You'll make a good houseboy. I might as well use you to make life a little easier."

When Mai Mai turned to go, Carnahan added, "Next time I'll teach you some more English, boy. This singsong language of yours is getting on my nerves. How old are you again, boy?"

"Fourteen."

"You have a boy's voice, but you are big for your age. So you can cook, eh?"

"Yes."

"If you can't, I'll throw you into the mines with the others. You are big enough to dig, I suppose."

When Carnahan returned to his map Mai Mai put the rag away and started for the door. "Oh, another thing, boy," Carnahan shouted after her, "wash your face once in a while. That dirty face of yours spoils my appetite."

Mai Mai returned to the deck, feeling more resentful. "Just wait until I am a woman again!" she told herself.

On the deck the villagers clustered around the body of Toy Sing and listened quietly to Mr. Quon, who stood a few feet away from them, speaking softly, his face sad.

"I promise you," he said, "Toy's body will be returned to his family in China with all expenses paid. It is unfortunate that he passed away before he earned any gold, but a man's life and death are predestined. Nobody can alter them except the almighty Jade Emperor in heaven. Now you can dress the body and wrap him in his own blanket and leave in it whatever message you wish to send to his family. We shall take care of the rest."

With a bow and a sad smile Mr. Quon limped away and disappeared into the cabin.

The next morning the boat reached a wide bottomland with oaks. The sun shone brightly on the green land dotted with tents. Mr. Quon came out and announced that they had reached the city of Sacramento, the first leg of the trip to the gold country. The gold mines were fifty miles farther east and they would start for the mines as soon as they disembarked.

The boat edged in among other boats and ships with tall masts, many of which were moored to the oak trees. On the bank, behind the trees, canvas structures were arranged in rows like streets. Mr. Carnahan and Mr. Gordon were the first ones to leap ashore. Mr. Quon followed a moment later, when the ship was securely tied to a tree. Mr. Carnahan hired six oxcarts and directed the cart drivers to unload the provisions immediately.

The Chinese waited in a dusty open space while the mule carts were being loaded, some squatting and some sitting on their bundles. Nearby many bearded miners were pitching tents, spreading blankets and unpacking pots and pans.

Both Mr. Carnahan and Mr. Quon were busy helping the drivers tie the large crates and bales on the carts. Mai Mai watched Carnahan resentfully, wondering if he beat his wife. Or did he have a wife? If he had, where was she? Was she pretty?

"Wei, Straw Sandal," Longevity said, "do you think Mr. Quon really has a wooden leg?"

"Knock on it and find out," she said.

"Hey, boy," Carnahan called, gesturing to Mai Mai. "Come here. You too, Longevity."

"Yes, sir!" Longevity said, jumping to his feet eagerly. Mai Mai followed him. "Go get my boots and suitcase," Mr. Carnahan ordered. "They are on the bunk in the cabin."

Both Mai Mai and Longevity went back to the *Sea Gull*. They arrived in time to see something that made them both gasp. The two men, Mr. King and Mr. Gordon, had just carried Toy Sing's body over the railing and were dumping it into the river.

"What are you two doing here?" Mr. King asked.

Longevity stared at him, not knowing what to say. Mai Mai, frightened by King's angry glare, began to back away. King leaped forward and grabbed her by the front of her coolie blouse. "Listen," he warned, "you didn't see anything, understand?"

Mr. Gordon quickly dug out two large gold coins from his pocket and stuffed one into Longevity's hand and the other into Mai Mai's. "This is to shut you up."

By this time Mr. King had taken out a bowie knife from his belt. He pointed it at Mai Mai's throat and told her that if she should tell anyone what she had just seen, he would cut her throat and dump her corpse into the river.

"That goes for you too," Mr. Gordon said to Longevity, almost lifting him up by his collar. Longevity stammered something; Mai Mai couldn't tell whether it was Chinese or English.

"You understand me, don't you?" King asked.

Mai Mai could feel the steely knife still jabbing at her throat. She swallowed hard and nodded. "All right," King said, letting her go. "See that you two keep your mouths shut."

9

The road became narrower and the villagers formed a single line. Refreshed after the tedious boat journey, everybody walked with a little bounce, eyes shining with expectation and the excitement of approaching the gold country.

Mai Mai had never seen such beautiful countryside before. The grass was even greener than rice shoots in the best years in Heavenly Tranquillity. Everything was big—the trees, the mountains, the rocks. . . . A toad that leaped across the road looked like a rabbit. Only the sun and the moon did not look different.

Longevity walked ahead of her restlessly, searching for wild berries and picking up rocks. Mai Mai watched the rolling hills covered with wild flowers of orange, blue, white, and purple, and thought of that large toad. It was in such a hurry. Was it a male toad going to find another toad? If it was, were they together now, she wondered. She inhaled deeply the fresh country air.

The road ahead turned and she could see the lead ox, which pulled the heaviest cart. Mr. Quon rode on it beside the driver, his back straight and his hands in his sleeves. He turned occasionally to tell the villagers of life in the camp and to give them some fatherly advice.

"If anyone teases you or pulls your pigtail, let him," he said. "Smile and say nothing. If anyone puts out a hand to you, shake it. It is a form of greeting in this foreign land, not a fighting gesture as you would normally think in China."

"I'm going to like it here," Longevity said, hitching up his trousers.

"Longevity," Mai Mai said, "have you ever wished you were a toad?"

"A toad? Why a toad? That's an ugly frog."

"It doesn't matter. A toad is beautiful in the eyes of another toad."

He picked up a rock and threw it at a tree. A bull's eye. "I wish I had a gun and a horse," he said.

"I wish your wish would come true, Longevity."

"I wish yours wouldn't. Who wants to be a toad?"

Before noon the caravan reached Sutter's Fort. It looked a little like a walled city with high gates, situated beside a beautiful oak park. Inside the walls were shops and a large square where people milled around. Half-naked men came and went with heavy burdens on their backs.

Mr. Quon pointed out that those were tamed Indians employed by Mr. Sutter to unload merchandise for his various shops in the fort. Mai Mai examined the Indians from a safe distance and was disappointed that they were not crimson. Four-eyed Dog explained that it was because they did not eat enough human heads.

When the caravan started again, it was already afternoon. The sun felt bright and warm in the cloudless sky. A faint, pale moon was hanging on one side. Mai Mai remembered that her mother had used to say, "When the sun and the moon come out to face each other, be happy. It is a good sign, for the moon goddess is in a good mood; she wants to be friendly with the Jade Emperor in heaven, who lives in the sun." And her mother would look at the moon and smile and add, "The day will come when the two will unite; then they will shower blessings upon earth."

Her mother had waited all her life for such a day, but it never came. Mai Mai had decided that the Jade Emperor was particular. However, she looked at the moon and smiled as her mother used to, and secretly urged the moon goddess to do her best.

"What are you staring at the sky for?" Longevity asked. "You've stepped on something dirty."

As Mai Mai cleaned her shoes of horse manure on the roadside grass, a large group of miners overtook the caravan again, singing loudly. It was a pretty song. She had heard it before. Now that the song had become more familiar she liked it even better. She joined the miners in the song softly and beat time with her hands as the miners rode by singing:

Oh, Susannah, don't you cry for me!
I'm off to California with my wash bowl on my knee!
I soon shall be in mining camps,
And then I'll look around,
And when I see the gold dust there,
I'll pick it off the ground.
I'll scrape the mountains clean, old girl,
I'll drain the rivers dry;
I'm off for California.
Oh, Susannah, don't you cry!

10

The caravan trudged along the narrow dusty road beside a small river that Mr. Quon called the American River. Birds were singing merrily among the lush trees. On the hills on one side Mai Mai recognized many bushes—the mountain laurel, the dogwood, and the buckthorn. In the distance she saw the long-needled pine rising here and there above the brush. The narrow river ran down a ravine, winding like a long, slender wriggling snake. The water foamed over rapids, and along the road was an occasional log cabin or tent.

The trip took two days. Before dusk the next day the caravan reached a good-sized hill with a lush growth of pines. Mr. Quon turned and announced that they were approaching the mines. Around the corner, true enough, the scenery suddenly changed. In the ravine the river widened, and in the dry bottom a large group of men, mostly in red shirts, worked like busy ants, digging and shoveling dirt out of trenches. Nearby, clinging to the hillside, were numerous white tents and log cabins. Presently the caravan reached a busy street lined with cabins and a few large wooden buildings. Mr. Quon again announced that they had arrived at Hangtown and that their claims were only two hundred yards upstream.

Without stopping, the caravan took a dusty path that led to the riverbed where many miners were working. Mr. Carnahan met them with a broad smile. He talked to Mr. Quon briefly, who then announced that they had reached the claims and he wanted everybody to help pitch tents at the foot of the hill. Mr. Carnahan had already unloaded the horses, which were hitched to a tall bush beside some jagged rocks.

"We shall have a rest and some food first," Mr. Quon said, busily passing out bread and biscuits. "Tomorrow morning we shall show you how to wash for gold and we'll have meat and rice for breakfast. We have brought smoked pork, which tastes like Cantonese smoked pork. You can begin to cook your own meals in the evening, when the day's work is done."

Four-eyed Dog, who had salted fish in mind, asked Mr. Quon if there were fish in the river. Mr. Quon told him he would be too busy digging gold to fish. Mr.

Carnahan, who understood some Chinese, added with good humor that if the diggings were good, he might buy some salted fish in San Francisco for Four-eyed Dog to fry. He said the stink might very well drive all the other miners away so that they could have the whole river to themselves.

The carts were quickly unloaded. Eleven tents were pitched in a row at the foot of the hill. Ta Ming, Longevity, Mai Mai, Catfish Cheong, Split-lip Lee, Four-eyed Dog, Old Wong and Chospstick Lew shared one tent. It was getting dark. Lights began to gleam in other tents that dotted the bank and the hills. In the fading twilight, columns of cooking smoke were seen curling up toward the starlit sky.

Everybody went to bed early. Mai Mai slept so soundly that, for the first time, she did not hear anybody snore. The next morning Mr. Quon arrived at dawn. He called the villagers together before breakfast and took them to the river to watch half a dozen men work. The miners carried iron pans full of earth to the waterside. They submerged them and let the lighter earth float off, then slopped the remainder over the side with a twisting motion until the gold and the black sand remained. The miners moved mechanically and they looked dull and grouchy. Mr. Quon didn't stop long enough to say anything to them.

He then took the villagers to a larger group of men who washed gold on a larger scale. They poured earth and water into a shallow wooden cradle on rockers. One husky, hairy-chested man, stripped to his waist, rocked the cradle violently, spilling water and mud over the side. "Don't ever drink cow's milk," Four-eyed

Dog said to Longevity. "If you do, you will grow hair like his on your chest."

Presently gold began to gleam in the black sand that was caught in the cleats at the bottom of the cradle. The hairy-chested man proudly showed a handful of the mixture to everybody as though it were a medal that he had just earned through some heroic deed. Mai Mai had never seen real gold before. She stared at it, spellbound, her heart thumping with excitement. Longevity kept mumbling a dirty exclamation he had learned from the seamen on the *Shooting Star*.

"You can say that again, boy," the miner said to Longevity, beaming with pride.

When they went back to the tents, Mr. Carnahan had already laid out the equipment on the ground—pails, shovels, picks, and pans. He taught everybody the movement of panning. He said that he had hired carpenters to build three large cradles. When they were ready he expected that the production would be tripled and that nobody would have to pan anymore. Digging was hard work, he added, but panning was the most tedious. So the cradles would be a welcome sight at the camp.

"Practice," he said. "Remember, every grain of gold that escapes the pan, you lose ten per cent of it."

As everybody concentrated on whirling and twisting his pan, Mr. Carnahan went around and corrected mistakes. Four-eyed Dog, the cook of the day, kept sneaking smoked pork into his mouth while nobody was looking.

Mai Mai sympathized with those who could not learn. A farmer called Ah Lum was the worst. After correcting him a dozen times, Mr. Carnahan gave up with a shrug. "This one is only good for digging," he said to Mr. Quon. "Hope nobody has to teach him to do that." But on the whole he was satisfied; he put out his thumb at those who learned easily, and praised, "*Tin qua qua!*"

The villagers practiced until Four-eyed Dog announced breakfast. Mr. Carnahan mounted his horse and rode away hurriedly as if he couldn't stand the sight or smell of whatever Four-eyed Dog had cooked.

Breakfast was served on the ground. The coolies squatted in circles and ate it, for the first time, with chopsticks and rice bowls. It was a good meal. Everybody was hungry for the steaming hot rice, which they blew noisily and shoveled into their mouths with their chopsticks. While eating, everybody smiled and looked happy except Four-eyed Dog, who squatted under a tree belching and looking groggy from overeating.

"*Wei,* Four-eyed Dog," Old Wong said, "why don't you eat? Don't you like your own cooking?"

"I'm eating," Four-eyed Dog said. He threw a piece of smoked pork into his mouth and chewed it slowly, his face almost purple. He swallowed the meat cross-eyed, and belched loudly.

Mr. Quon, who ate with them, told everybody to eat as much as possible, for they were going to spend the whole morning digging. Lunch would be foreign bread and water, which Four-eyed Dog would bring to the hills at noon. He would also bring some American cheese just in case anybody had learned to eat it. The word cheese made quite a few men wrinkle their noses as though they had smelled something bad. "I remember eating it on that foreign ship," Four-eyed Dog said, making a face. "Uh, now I have lost appetite for another bowl of rice."

"Think of salted fish," Old Wong advised.

As soon as the breakfast was over everybody got up quickly and picked up the tools, eager to start digging. At this moment Mr. Carnahan returned on his white horse and held a brief conference with Mr. Quon. "All right," Mr. Quon said in Cantonese, "you all follow me. A pick, a shovel and a pail are what you need this morning. Not the pan."

When Mai Mai picked up the equipment, she heard Mr. Carnahan shout at her, "Hey, boy, not you! You come with me."

11

Mr. Carnahan rode quietly. Mai Mai walked briskly behind him, trying to keep pace with his horse. She wondered what Mr. Carnahan was thinking and where he was taking her. She wanted to go with him, but on the other hand she was also disappointed that she couldn't go to the hills with the others. She had worked up a great enthusiasm about digging gold.

She watched Mr. Carnahan's erect back as she almost trotted, trying to keep up with his horse. Presently the dusty trail went around the hill. She saw numerous tents and two taller buildings behind the oak trees. The scene seemed familiar. Suddenly she realized it was the town called Hangtown she had passed through the day before.

The tent street was almost deserted now except for some people in the larger buildings; a few loitered in front of the general store next to the saloon. Mr. Carnahan rode through the street without saying a word or looking to his right or left. Mai Mai wondered if he had forgotten that she was following him. When he reached a log cabin at the end of the short street he dismounted. "This is where you work every day, boy," he said, hitching the horse to a post beside the cabin. "Come in."

Inside the dark, small cabin the air was stuffy. Mr. Carnahan threw open the shutters and the morning sun immediately flooded into the room, casting a dusty beam on a crude, unpainted table that was cluttered with mugs and dishes. Hanging over the table was a hurricane lamp. The three benches had been pushed under the table to make room for passage around it. Behind the table was the kitchen, equipped with a potbellied stove, a cutting board, a few pails and another bench piled with dirty pots and pans. On the other side of the room were a double bunk and a single bed. The double bunk was strewn with clothes but the single bed was neat and tidy. Mr. Carnahan opened a side door that had two strong locks, and stepped in.

"This is my room and office," he said. "Come in."

The smaller room was furnished with a bed, a desk and two chairs. In a corner was a strongbox, again with two locks. Beside the chest was Mr. Carnahan's collection of boots, neatly placed in a row. Four rifles and two gun belts hung on the wall above the chest. Mr. Carnahan picked up a pair of black boots, blew the dust off them and cleaned a dirty spot with a wet finger. "Here, take the mud off the heels," he said, handing the boots to Mai Mai. "That's your first daily duty. Keep those boots clean and shiny."

Mai Mai counted the boots. There were nine pairs: three yellow, three red and three black. "Rags and polish are in this box," Mr. Carnahan said, picking out from the wooden box a velvet rag. He put a foot on a chest and started shining the black boots he was wearing. "In case of fire, save the chest first, then my boots, understand?"

Mai Mai understood most of it except the word "fire." Mr. Carnahan cleared that up easily with a little gesture of the hands. "You are a clever boy," he said. "I don't see any future trouble in communication. Now, after you've shined the boots, sweep the floor and tidy up the bed. I don't give a damn how it looks outside, but I want this room kept clean, understand? Spotless clean! And don't touch those guns. They are loaded and I don't want any fool to shoot a hole in his own head. Hey, boy, have you forgotten something?"

Mai Mai was puzzled for a moment. "Say 'yes, sir' if you understand me," Mr. Carnahan went on. "That's the only way for me to check where we stand. I don't want to waste a lot of breath on an order while you think I'm telling you a funny story. Understand?"

"Yes, sir," Mai Mai said.

"Then wipe that puzzled look off your face. And I don't want any big silly grin, either. A Chinaman's grin doesn't mean anything. Nobody can make out if it means 'yes' or 'no' anyhow. When you're through with this room, go to the other room and see what you can do about it. It's filthy. The only thing that is clean is Mr. Quon's bed. The double bunk belongs to Mr. King and Mr. Gordon. They will be back in a few days. Tidy it up. And throw those dirty clothes into the box beside it. Fold them if you have time. Mr. King won't know the difference, but it will be easier on my eyes. The moment I step out of this room, the first thing I see is that damned bunk and those dirty clothes. Understand me, boy?"

Mai Mai stared at him, puzzled. "Never mind," Mr. Carnahan went on, "start working. Shine those boots first. One thing at a time. You'll learn the language fast enough. One of these days I'll buy you a shirt. You can get rid of that ragged coolie blouse and look decent." He stared at her and frowned. "Boy, do you ever wash your face?"

"Yes, sir," Mai Mai said.

"Scrub it a little harder next time," Mr. Carnahan said. He went to his desk and busied himself with some paper work.

While Mai Mai shined the boots she cast an occasional glance at him, wondering if this was his permanent home. She hoped it was. She liked the cabin. There was a great deal of work to be done. And there was no other woman in the cabin to tell her what to do. There were other advantages too. In the privacy of the cabin she could bathe herself and do a lot of other things she had been longing to do.

Mr. Carnahan was busy for a while, concentrating on

his work. He opened his chest twice. Each time he took something out and put something in. He acted as though nobody else was in the room. Mai Mai, shining the boots on the ground, wondered what was in the chest. She argued with herself whether she should take a peek. "No, I mustn't look," she told herself. But the more she forbade herself to look the more curious she became.

Before she finished shining all the boots Mr. Carnahan locked his chest and his drawers and put on his hat. "I'll be back in two hours," he said. "When I come back, I want to see this place looking different." He left hurriedly.

Through the window Mai Mai watched him mount his white horse and gallop away. It was wonderful to have some privacy. She felt like throwing herself on the bed, kicking and giggling. But she did not have time for silly girlish behavior. She first poured herself a basin of water and sprinkled the fresh cool water on her face— not too much, just enough to wet her skin. She enjoyed the water creeping slowly down her chin.

Then she took a towel and dried it. A few drops fell onto the adobe ground. She sprinkled some more water on herself and in a mirror over the washbasin, watched the water creep down. She slanted the mirror at such an angle that she could see her profile. How wonderful it would be if she could leap onto the street now and tell the whole world that she was really a girl, not a dirty little coolie boy!

She heard the sound of horse hooves. Horrified, she quickly smoothed her hair. But the noise faded away. She looked at herself in the mirror again. She hadn't seen her own real face for so long that she wondered if it had changed. She looked at herself closely. She hadn't changed, except that she looked healthier. The good food she had eaten on the *Shooting Star* must have contributed the nice color to her cheeks. She wetted her hair and smoothed it, then looked at herself from a different angle. Yes, she was still the same girl who had always turned men's heads on the streets in Heavenly Tranquillity.

Satisfied, she once again dirtied her face with the bit of half-burned wood she carried in her pocket. She had wasted enough time now. Biting her tongue she plunged into work. She wiped and scrubbed, and before noon everything in the cabin looked tidy and clean.

While waiting for Mr. Carnahan to return, she gave his boots an extra shining. "If this doesn't make him smile a little," she thought, "I'll shine his face too, with his boot polish." Then she wiped the heavy chest once more. Again she wondered what was in it. With a smile she sat on it gingerly, hugged herself and indulged in a little wild thought. She pretended she was in China, sitting on a chest, waiting for her husband—perhaps it was Ta Ming—to come home for supper, a chest full of gold, brought back from the Land of the Golden Mountain.

12

✻ At the camp, at night, Mai Mai heard the villagers talk about nothing but gold. For almost two weeks now they had been obsessed by gold fever, talking and digging and washing the pay dirt from dawn to dusk. They kept the mixture of black sand and gold dust in canvas bags worn around their waists. At the end of a day's work they handed the bags to Mr. Quon for weighing and safekeeping. Each worker was anxious to know how much gold he had already mined, and made new plans for his future—what rice fields to buy, what houses to build and how to beautify his ancestral burial grounds.

Old Wong had the most ambitious plans of all. He wanted to move to Canton, the capital city of Kwantung Province, and open the largest slaughterhouse in China. He would take a young concubine to boost the prestige of his wife. The concubine would be subservient to both his wife and himself, besides bearing for him at least five more children. That would make his offspring a round ten, a lucky number. He would then hire the best Confucian scholar in Canton to teach his children the manners of the Mandarin. The sons, preferably in the majority, would all pass the Imperial Examination in Peking and receive appointments from the Emperor. The daughters—two or three would be enough—could all embroider and write poetry. They should all be virtuous and not too smart, a standard set by Confucius. They would all be married to young men of his choice along with a handsome dowry; and when they were carried to their new homes in bridal sedan chairs they would all cry real tears, as required by the customs of high society. They must not behave like those country maidens who could hardly wait to get married.

As for himself, he would retire at the age of fifty, enjoy his leisure, the attention and respect of his grandchildren, preferably numbered at forty, all told. And eventually, when death came, at about sixty or so, he would be buried with the most elaborate funeral in Canton. Then he would be able to arrive in the other world and meet his dead ancestors with great pride.

When Old Wong talked about his reunion with his dead ancestors, his face shone and eyes sparkled. Everybody watched him enviously. "A long life is desirable," Old Wong philosophized, puffing on his long bamboo pipe contentedly, "but death is the happy end of a long journey. Every year, during the ancestral festival, if you have eight filial sons and two virtuous daughters to burn incense at your grave, what more can a man ask? Eh, I ask you!"

Everybody was in full agreement with Old Wong, nodding and repeating the same question to one another.

"What is your ambition, Longevity?" Four-eyed Dog asked.

"First I want to learn the foreign talk well," Longevity said. "Then I want to learn how to shoot and ride a horse."

Four-eyed Dog winced. "What's yours, Straw Sandal?"

Mai Mai knew what her ambition was but she wouldn't tell. She cast Ta Ming a quick glance and blushed slightly. "I want to touch gold," she said. "And sleep on it."

"You are not digging," Four-eyed Dog said. "How are you going to get your ten percent?"

"I'm going to dig," Mai Mai said.

"Me too," Longevity said.

"What if the foreigners won't let you?"

"I can talk the foreign talk."

"What if they say, 'Hey boy, your mouth still smells of your mother's milk. Wait two or three years when you start eating solid food.' What are you going to say to that, eh?"

"Damn you," Longevity said in English.

Four-eyed Dog turned away with a wince. "Foreign talk, *pei!*"

The next day Mai Mai went to work early and did her job with extra care and thoroughness. By the time Mr. Carnahan returned, the log cabin was meticulously clean, his boots were lying neatly in a row, shining like honor guards waiting for inspection. Today she had a great favor to ask Mr. Carnahan.

"Sir," she said in English. "Sir, I beg something from you, yes?"

"What's on your mind, boy?" Mr. Carnahan asked, going to his desk to do his usual paper work.

"Your boots look pretty today, sir?"

Carnahan glanced at his boots. "A fine job. Excellent. Keep at it."

"Yes, sir." She waited for a moment, then went on. "Tomorrow I dig gold. Yes, sir?"

Carnahan looked up with a scowl. "What?"

Mai Mai repeated what she had just said.

"Is the work in this cabin too light for you, boy?"

"I want dig. I can dig much gold. I am strong."

Carnahan stared at her. Suddenly he got up, went to Mai Mai, grabbed her pigtail and turned her face up. "I told you to wash your face. Why didn't you, boy?"

"Next time, I wash," Mai Mai said, trying not to stammer. "I go dig tomorrow, all right?"

Carnahan stared at her for a long time. Mai Mai, grabbing the corners of her coolie blouse, stared back boldly, wondering what he wanted.

Suddenly Carnahan let her pigtail go. "All right," he said. "You may appreciate the soft job in this cabin after you've acquired a few blisters. You can work here in the mornings and go digging in the afternoon. Go now. See if you like it better."

"Now?"

"Yes, now."

When Mai Mai got back to the camp she wondered why Mr. Carnahan had stared at her face like that for so long. Was he suspicious of her sex? Or had he wondered about her age? She had not time to worry about that now. The prospect of digging and panning for gold excited her more every day. Had she also caught gold fever like the others? Or was she anxious to work beside Ta Ming? She didn't know. Suddenly that soothing picture returned to her mind—the picture of herself sitting on a chest of gold waiting for Ta Ming to come home for supper. She quickened her steps.

At the camp she picked a pail and a shovel and rushed to the mines in the hills. She found Ta Ming's mine. He was shoveling dirt out of a four-foot deep trench beside a few others, their heads popping in and out, perspiration flying. Longevity was digging too. Everybody seemed to have caught gold fever. Mai Mai leaped into the trench and plunged into work.

The sun poured down on her. Presently perspiration ran down her face and her hands blistered. But she kept hacking the dirt away feverishly. Then she shoveled the dirt into her pail as though every bit of it were pure gold.

"Throw the soft dirt away," Ta Ming shouted at her. "There is no gold in the top layer."

"Yes, sir," Mai Mai answered in English, forgetting that she was talking to Ta Ming. She tossed the dirt out like the others and went deeper until she hit a layer of coarse sand. She filled her pail with it and dashed to the river.

At the river she discovered she didn't have a pan. She dashed back and borrowed one. Ta Ming watched her, shaking his head, half amused and half worried.

Mai Mai panned her dirt breathlessly, her heart pounding. She rocked and twisted the submerged pan until the mud was washed away. When she brought it out of the water and examined the contents, there was nothing left but coarse sand and some pebbles. Disappointed, she threw it away, dashed back to the trench and resumed her digging like a tireless beaver. Ta Ming came over to her, still shaking his head.

"Go deeper," he advised. "Dig four feet, at least. You can only find gold in the bluish clay. Here, go wash this." He dumped beside her a pail of the heavier dirt.

Mai Mai had no time to talk. She grabbed it and made a dash for the river. Just as she was about to reach the water she tripped over a rock and scattered the contents of her pail wide and far. In spite of a painful toe and bruised knees and hands, she scrambled to her feet and raced back to the trench.

"Go easy, Straw Sandal," Ta Ming said, more worried than amused now. "The gold is here. It is not going to run away."

Mai Mai filled the pail with the dirt and once more dashed back to the river, her clothes wet with perspiration and her pigtail flying. She panned the dirt excitedly, her eyes strained over the shallow water, searching for the first glow of gold. The moment she discovered a tiny fleck among the black sand in her pan she let out a cry that startled Longevity, who was panning beside her.

"What's the matter, Straw Sandal?" Longevity asked. "Bitten by a crab?"

"Gold!"

Longevity looked and made a face. "You have enough in that pan to fill a small fingernail."

"How much have you panned?"

"Enough to fill ten large fingernails, at least."

"Then I have no time to talk," she said, racing back for more pay dirt. She forgot the heat, the painful toe and the bruises. She worked feverishly until after dusk and collected a small sack of black sand with some gold flecks in it. When Mr. Quon came to collect the gold she asked him if she could keep it for a night. She wanted to sleep on it for luck. Mr. Quon looked at the meager contents of the sack and said with a shrug, "Enough to buy a toothpick. Keep it."

The remark didn't cure her of gold fever. Back at the tent she could not take her eyes off her gold. She fingered it, squeezed it and bounced it on her palm. "*Wei,* Straw Sandal," Four-eyed Dog said, "why don't you smell it and chew it? That's the only thing you haven't done so far."

Longevity, who had also been allowed to keep his, was tucking his small sackful under his pillow. "It is not black sand," he said to Four-eyed Dog. "It is gold."

"It is not gold until you have blown the sand away.

Do you want me to blow it for you? I know how. I watched the foreigners do it."

"How?" Longevity asked.

"Just flip it in the air and blow it."

"I don't believe you."

"Ask your father."

Longevity asked his father. Ta Ming nodded. "I am not going to blow mine until I have learned how," Longevity said.

"Straw Sandal," Old Wong suggested, "blow yours. Let's all take a look at your pure gold. We won't have ours until the end of the month."

Somewhat dubiously Mai Mai poured the sand in a pan and proceeded to blow it. She did it gingerly at first. When all the sand fell back into the pan she blew a little stronger. She repeated the process a few times but no sand was blown away. She began to feel dizzy.

"Let Four-eyed Dog help," Old Wong advised. "He has the biggest mouth and the strongest lung power, acquired through talking."

Four-eyed Dog acknowledged the compliment with a nod. He offered his services to Mai Mai in exchange for whatever delicacy Mai Mai could borrow from Mr. Carnahan's cabin.

But Mai Mai would not let anyone blow her gold. She kept blowing it herself, increasing her power with every breath. Presently her face became red and her head began to swim, but she finally succeeded in getting rid of the black sand.

"Did I tell you?" Longevity said. "Just enough to fill a small fingernail."

Mai Mai watched her pinch of gold with fascination. "But it's pure gold!" she said breathlessly.

"Well, sleep on it," Four-eyed Dog suggested.

After dinner Mai Mai put her gold under her pillow and slept on it. Her gold fever subsided and she slept wonderfully well that night.

13

The next morning Mai Mai went to work with a cold, a limp, plus burning bruises on her knees and blisters on her hands. When Mr. Carnahan saw her, he burst out laughing. "Well, have you been in a fight, boy?"

Mai Mai said she got all this from digging gold. "Just as I told you, boy," Mr. Carnahan said. "A horse doesn't enjoy hay until it has chewed the prickly tumbleweed. Now, go back to the nice soft job—shine my boots. Oh, I forgot. I bought you a shirt. Put it on."

He picked up a shirt from his bed and handed it to Mai Mai. "Take those rags off your back," he added. "Nothing looks more ridiculous than a Chinaman's coolie blouse."

Mai Mai quickly put on the shirt. "I said take that damned coolie blouse off," Mr. Carnahan ordered. "You can't wear the nice new shirt over that!"

When Mai Mai refused, Carnahan peeled the new shirt off and made an attempt to undress her. Terrified, she struggled free and fled the cabin. In one breath she ran to the oak tree in the middle of the street. She leaned on the tree and panted, then peeked at Mr. Carnahan from behind the tree. Mr. Carnahan had mounted his horse and was galloping away in the opposite direction. She didn't know what to do. Mr. Carnahan was the only man who had suspected that she was a woman. It worried her and excited her at the same time. But it made her feel like a woman again, a woman torn between wanting and fear. She had always been attracted to Ta Ming; now suddenly she found Mr. Carnahan more attractive. Ta Ming had never paid much attention to her and had never looked at her as anything but a dirty coolie boy. Mr. Carnahan had grabbed her pigtail, turned up her face and stared at her strangely for a long time the other day. And today he had tried to undress her. His suspicion seemed to her the only compliment she had received since she had left China. As she thought of it she found herself staring at the cabin, her heart pounding, her cheeks burning.

Back in the cabin she shined all Mr. Carnahan's

boots with extra care in spite of her blistered hands. Then she tidied up his room, washed the windows and the mirror. When she caught her own reflection in the mirror, she stared at it, visualizing it in a beautiful gown of blue silk, a delicate folding fan in one hand and a lotus flower in the other. She tipped her head slightly to one side and smiled, striking the pose of the lotus goddess. Then she touched her dimpled cheek with a forefinger, turned her head sideways and glanced at the mirror with a conquettish smile, imagining she was smiling at Mr. Carnahan.

When she finished cleaning Mr. Carnahan's room she went to the outer room. She found, to her surprise, that the double bunk had been slept in. She wondered if Mr. Carnahan had had visitors. Or had Mr. King and Mr. Gordon returned?

She looked into the wooden crates beside the bunk and discovered the folded clothes were now covered with other dirty clothes. She did not have to ask. Mr. King and Mr. Gordon were back. Suddenly she felt a chill, and all her romantic feelings about men vanished.

She dutifully cleaned the cabin and washed the dishes and mugs scattered on the table, feeling ashamed and foolish.

Before noon Mr. Carnahan returned with Mr. Gordon and Mr. King, two more mule carts of new supplies and three more horses. With the help of the two Mexican mule drivers, they unloaded the carts and carried the large sacks into the cabin and piled them in a corner. "Boy," Mr. Carnahan said to Mai Mai, "You know Mr. King and Mr. Gordon."

"What is he doing here?" Mr. King asked with a

slight frown. He looked darker and thinner, his eyes bloodshot.

"He's worth more as a houseboy," Mr. Carnahan said. "This place used to be a messy chicken coop. Now it's livable. It's good for the spirit. Besides, he makes good coffee. Boy, go boil some water. See if you can make even better coffee. And don't sneeze in that coffee pot!"

While waiting for coffee, Mr. Carnahan and his partners smoked and discussed the mine operations. Mr. Carnahan had staked more claims up the river. The present diggings were not too satisfactory. It seemed to him a waste of labor. Now that they had more supplies, he favored a bigger gamble.

"What do you mean, bigger gamble?" Mr. King asked.

"I mean go deeper," Mr. Carnahan said. "The surface pay dirt is all gone. There is nothing worth washing in the first five feet. A group of native Californians hit a strike the other day farther up the river. They dug fifteen feet before they made that lucky strike. They dug out nuggets as big as your thumb."

"Fifteen feet?" Mr. Gordon said. "That's impossible. We ain't gophers."

"That's exactly what I aim to do—dig down like the gophers," Mr. Carnahan said. "If the Californians can do it, we can do it, too."

"Yes," Mr. King said. "And we got the manpower to do it. Chinamen are good diggers. Or are they?"

"Work harder than mules, and don't kick," Mr. Carnahan said.

"What have we got to lose?" Mr. King said. "We

don't pay them nothing if we don't find gold. That's in the contract. I'm with you, John. It's worth the gamble. And we've got plenty of food. Enough for at least a two-month operation."

"What do you think, Gordon?" Mr. Carnahan asked.

"Well, it's pretty risky," Mr. Gordon said.

"What do we care, man?" Mr. King said. "John can go back to his ranch in the midwest and you and I can always go back to piloting old ferry boats if we go broke."

"Everything is a gamble, boys," Mr. Carnahan said. "I can't go back to the ranch. I sold it to gamble on this. I'll talk to Quon about it."

"Quon?" Mr. King said. "Is he still with us?"

"I mean to keep him. He's my partner. Got money in this operation."

"But the Chinaman don't dig. Said it's below his dignity."

"We've got a hundred and six other Chinamen digging for us," Mr. Carnahan said. "Besides, in this business muscles alone are not enough. Money and brains are just as important. And a lot of good luck. The inscrutable Oriental may have it. He was a lucky gambler once."

"All right, John," Mr. King said, spitting out a mouthful of tobacco juice and hitting a brass cuspidor six feet away. "You're the boss. I ain't got no objection to this Chinaman, provided he makes some contribution to this operation. Still I prefer a white partner. This Chinaman makes me mighty uncomfortable. One of these days I'm going to shoot off those long fingernails of his. They give me the jitters. Hey, where are those horses we bought?"

They leaped to the window and looked. The three unsaddled horses, which had been tied to a post beyond Mr. Carnahan's, were gone.

"Stolen," Mr. Carnahan said. He rushed to the hitching post and examined the ground. There was nothing but a few droppings. "Can't tell which way they've gone," he went on. "Might be to the east. Go borrow McGowen's horses and follow me. Can't be too far." He quickly unhitched his spirited white horse, leaped onto it and galloped away.

Both Mr. King and Mr. Gordon rushed into the cabin, took their gun belts down from the wall and dashed out again. A few minutes later they galloped past the window toward the east, churning up a cloud of dust.

It was not until an hour later that Mai Mai heard the thumping of hooves outside the cabin. She rushed to the window to watch. Mr. Gordon returned first, covered with dust. He hitched the horse and came in, panting. Without a word he took a quick drink of water from a flask hanging on the wall, then brought out a coil of rope from under the double bunk and hurried out again. Just then horses' hooves thundered. Mr. Carnahan arrived with two other mounted men, their hands tied behind their backs. Mr. King followed them with the three stolen horses.

"I've got the rope," Mr. Gordon said.

"Can't hang them yet," Mr. Carnahan said. "They're entitled to a trial."

"Since when do we try horse thieves?" Mr. King

said, dismounting. "Let's string 'em up before the rest of the gang shoots us to pieces. C'mon, Gordon, let's go!"

He grabbed the reins of the horses on which the two horse thieves were riding. Then he whipped out his gun and rode away. Mr. Gordon mounted his horse and followed with the rope.

Mr. Carnahan watched them go. Then, with a shrug, he tied the three horses to the post closer to the window and came into the cabin. "Pour me a cup of coffee, boy," he said.

While Mai Mai was pouring the coffee Mr. Carnahan brushed his clothes and changed his dusty boots.

"Guess I'll have to teach you how to shoot," Mr. Carnahan said. "This town isn't safe anymore. Have you handled a gun before, boy?"

Mai Mai looked puzzled. She wasn't too sure what he was talking about. Carnahan repeated the question with gestures.

"Yes, sir," Mai Mai said, shaking her head.

"You mean 'no, sir,'" Mr. Carnahan said. "Doggone it, don't confuse me."

He drew his gun and tossed it in the air. The gun made a somersault and landed in his hand again with the handle toward Mai Mai. "Take it and shoot. See if you can hit that hitching post over there."

Mai Mai took the gun. With a shaking hand she aimed it at the farther hitching post through the window. "Come over here," Mr. Carnahan said, opening the door. "Shoot through the door. I don't want you to kill my horses."

Her heart pounding, Mai Mai closed her eyes and pulled the trigger. The horses jumped.

"Missed the post by a mile," Mr. Carnahan said. "C'mon, I'll teach you. You ought to at least hit a barn after the first lesson."

They went to the square about a hundred yards from the cabin. Using an oak tree as a target Carnahan started the lesson without nonsense. His face serious and voice stern, he taught her how to hold the gun, how to draw and how to aim. Mai Mai practiced and fired at the oak tree five times, hitting the tree three times from a distance of thirty feet.

"Not bad, boy," Mr. Carnahan said. "At thirty feet you can hit a tree. You ought to be able to hit a man at half the distance."

Suddenly they heard two shots. Mr. Carnahan drew his other gun. "Take cover, boy," he said, dashing behind the oak tree. Mai Mai followed.

Mr. King and Mr. Gordon appeared around the corner, their guns drawn and their horses snorting. "Anything wrong?" Mr. King asked.

Mr. Carnahan stepped out from behind the oak tree. "I'm teaching the boy to shoot," he said, "just in case."

"Thought you and the rest of the horse thieves had started shooting," Mr. Gordon said. "That's why we rushed down."

"What happened to those two?" Mr. Carnahan asked.

"We strung 'em up," Mr. King said.

"And finished 'em before they had time to kick," Mr. Gordon said.

"You shot them?" Mr. Carnahan asked.

"Yeah, while they were dangling on the ropes. Don't want to take no chances."

"They're Ringo's boys," Mr. Carnahan said. "Hope you haven't brought us some royal headaches."

"I can hardly wait to have a talk with Ringo, with my gun," Mr. King said. "Any time, any place. Preferably near the claims so I can bury him without having to dig another hole."

"We'll do the same to Ringo," Mr. Gordon said. "String him up."

"You make it sound as easy as plucking a chicken for dinner," Mr. Carnahan said. "Well, no use worrying about it now. Let's go back and have some lunch."

14

Back at the camp, the Chinese had not returned from the mines. Ta Ming was cooking. Longevity was helping him, washing rice a few yards away from the stove. Mai Mai told him of what had happened in Hangtown and that she was learning how to shoot. "Let's go see the corpses," Longevity said excitedly.

Mai Mai took Longevity back to Hangtown, where the hanging had taken place. About fifty yards away from the tent street they saw a group of men standing around a large oak tree on which two bodies were dangling. The people, mostly miners in red shirts, talked and gesticulated.

"Let's go closer," Longevity suggested.

They went into the crowd, and when Mai Mai took a close look at the bodies, she covered her face in horror. Longevity stared at the dead men, fascinated, until he discovered that Mai Mai was no longer with him. He went out of the crowd and found her standing a few feet away, looking very sick.

"What's wrong?" he asked.

"Let's go home, Longevity. You can have my dinner tonight."

"I never saw such ugly dead bandits in my life," Longevity said. "They stared right into my eyes. Will you teach me how to shoot, Straw Sandal?"

"I never want to hold a gun again," Mai Mai said.

"Will Mr. Carnahan teach me?"

"I'll ask him."

It was almost dusk when they hurried back to the camp. During dinner the villagers talked about the dead horse thieves and began to worry. They decided to burn some incense and paper money for the Jade Emperor in heaven, asking the god to protect them from possible invasion of the two evil spirits. Since it was almost the end of the month, Mr. Quon might bring their pay at any time. They must do everything to keep the pay day a lucky occasion.

The mention of gold immediately lighted up everybody's face. The bodies of the robbers were promptly forgotten. Mai Mai's appetite returned and she finished her dinner. "Ai, pay day," Four-eyed Dog said, rubbing his hands eagerly. "Ai, have we been here a month already?"

"Twenty-one days," Ta Ming said.

"Ah, in nine days we shall have our own gold!"

Suddenly everybody started to talk simultaneously. Some guessed how much gold they were going to get; others discussed better ways to mine the gold; a few worried about the gold's safety. Catfish Cheong estimated a years's savings. He calculated how many acres of rice fields he could afford and how much he should put aside for taking a wife.

Chopstick Lew talked about his retirement to a Buddhist temple in the mountains. His greatest desire was to die in peace, preferably in his sleep. If not, he did not mind passing away while eating. Food was one of the great pleasures of life and he might as well enjoy it to the very end. Besides, to die with a full belly would guarantee a good life in the next world.

Four-eyed Dog agreed with him wholeheartedly. Old Wong, who did not like Chopstick too well, asked him, if he enjoyed food so much, why was he still so skinny?

Chopstick took offense. He made a few derogatory remarks about fat men and then launched into a long account of how well he had eaten when times were good. Everybody knew that Chopstick, being stingy, would not spend an extra coin on food. But nobody was willing to participate in a pointless discussion for fear of making Chopstick sick again. His loud groaning would spoil any happy day, if not actually attract evil spirits.

Nevertheless it was an exciting evening. Longevity went to bed thinking of shooting and riding a horse. Mai Mai, still haunted by the images of the dead horse thieves, decided to occupy her mind with something more pleasant. She thought of Mr. Carnahan.

The next day Longevity asked her to take him to Hangtown. He was determined to learn how to shoot. "Do you know why we have pigtails?" He asked as they started for Mr. Carnahan's cabin. "Because we are not Manchus. When the first Manchu Emperor came to China, he ordered all Chinese to grow pigtails so that his soldiers could grab our pigtails if we attempted to escape."

"Who told you that?" Mai Mai asked.

"My father. Do you know why Chinese women have small bound feet? Because the Manchu Emperor ordered all Chinese women to bind their feet. If the Chinese women attempted to escape, the Manchu soldiers could catch them easily. My father says one day the Chinese will rise again and drive the Manchus back to the wild mountains in Manchuria. That's why I want to learn how to shoot."

"Did your father tell you all that?"

"Yes. It is all true too."

"I am surprised that no magistrate arrested him and cut his head off."

"He is not stupid enough to tell that to just anybody. But he is not afraid."

"Can he shoot?"

"He can use a spear very well."

When they arrived at the cabin, Mr. Quon, Mr. King and Mr. Gordon had already left, leaving many dirty dishes and mugs on the table. Mai Mai and Longevity cleaned the outer room before Mr. Carnahan came out of his room. He looked at Longevity, somewhat surprised. "What are you doing here, boy?"

"He say he learn shooting, sir," Mai Mai said.

Longevity gave Mr. Carnahan a big smile. "I kill robber. Bang, bang, bang!"

"Not a bad idea," Mr. Carnahan said. "We can use another gunslinger, provided you can see straight. Here, take this gun. See if you have the strength to level it." He gave Longevity one of his two guns. Longevity stared at it wide-eyed for a moment. "Do you know how to load it, boy?"

"No, sir."

Mr. Carnahan inserted six bullets into his second gun with fast fingers. "See? It's easy. Now, load it a few times before the target practice." He handed the second gun to Mai Mai. "Try it."

Mai Mai took the gun and her hands began to shake. They both loaded their guns clumsily. Mr. Carnahan laughed. "The worst shot in town could shoot your heads full of holes if you're that slow, boys. But never mind. You've got no enemy. Not now, anyway. And you Chinamen have slender fingers. If they're as fast as your tongues when you talk that singsong language of yours, you'll make good gunslingers." He turned to Longevity. "C'mon, I'll teach you how to shoot. What's your name again?"

"Longevity."

"You need a name like that in this town, boy."

Mr. Carnahan took them to the square and gave Longevity the same lesson he had given Mai Mai the day before. Longevity was a natural shot; he hit the oak tree four times out of five. But Mai Mai could not shoot anymore. Every time she pulled the trigger her hands shook so badly that the bullet went wild. "Don't close your eyes, damn it," Mr. Carnahan said sharply. "How do you expect to hit anything if you shoot with your eyes closed?"

"I see blood if I don't close the eye," Mai Mai said.

"What blood?"

"I see blood come out of big hole."

"What big hole?" Carnahan asked, scowling.

Suddenly Mai Mai's face turned pale and she quickly threw her hand over her mouth as though she were going to throw up.

"Go back and shine my boots, boy," Carnahan said irritably. "You've wasted enough bullets. As for you, Longevity, I'll give you six bullets every day. Come to shoot at the oak tree about noon. That's when the town is deserted. I don't want you to kill anybody. If you did, they would sure come like a pack of wolves and string all of you up. The last thing I need is a bunch of dead Chinamen dangling in oak trees. All right, practice loading when you aren't shooting. Understand, boy?"

"Damn right," Longevity said.

Mr. Carnahan looked a little surprised, then laughed. "Well, don't talk tough so soon, boy. Wait till you can draw fast enough to hit a cow crossing the street, at least. Now go back and do some housework."

He took the gun from Mai Mai, juggled it and holstered it, then leaped on his horse and galloped away. Longevity watched him, his eyes wide with admiration.

"Hot damn!" he said in English, then in Chinese, "Wish I could ride like him."

"You will, Longevity," Mai Mai said. "Let's go back."

"I have six bullets, Straw Sandal. Let me use three before we go back. Tell me what you want me to hit."

"The small tree beyond the big one."

Longevity aimed at the small oak tree about a hundred yards away and fired. "Did I hit it?" he asked.

"I don't know," Mai Mai said. "But you frightened all the birds out of it."

A man came out of the saloon nearby, pulled out his gun and fired three shots into the air, laughing and yelling, "Yahoo!" Then he staggered drunkenly to his horse, climbed on it and promptly fell over the other side.

"Did you kill him?" Mai Mai asked fearfully.

"I couldn't have missed the tree by that much," Longevity said.

"Let's go back."

They hurried back to the cabin. After they had cleaned the cabin together, Longevity practiced loading the gun and juggling it. Then he put a bench beside the table and practiced mounting the table as if it were a horse, imitating Mr. Carnahan's every move. Mai Mai watched him, worrying.

15

In the afternoon Mr. Carnahan returned earlier than usual. Longevity had practiced juggling the gun more than an hour and when he handed the gun back to Mr. Carnahan, he juggled it. Mr. Carnahan snatched it away in midair.

"Don't learn any bad habits, boy," Carnahan said. "Guns are made for shooting, not juggling. I have this bad habit and almost got killed twice. Once by myself and once by an enemy who had already aimed his gun at my nose while I was still juggling. I wouldn't be here talking to you if he hadn't been such a rotten shot. But he shot my hat off and that frightened five years off my life." With a flourish he juggled the gun and holstered it. "That's all, boy. Come back tomorrow. I'll leave the gun on the table. Go shooting at the oak tree about noon, understand?"

"Yes, sir," Longevity said.

"That's the boy. Keep practicing. When you can hit that tree at a hundred yards, I might get you a cowboy hat and a pair of boots. I might as well make a gunman out of you. Now go home."

As Mai Mai started to follow Longevity, Mr. Carnahan grabbed her by the arm. "Not you, boy," he said. "There is more work to be done in this cabin."

After Longevity had left, Carnahan shoved her into his room, shut the door and locked it. "Put on that shirt I bought you," he commanded. "It's on the chest. Go ahead, put it on and get rid of that theatrical costume."

"I put on tomorrow," Mai Mai said.

Carnahan grabbed her arms suddenly, took her to the wash basin, forced her face down and started scrubbing it with soap and water. She struggled. A coin fell out of her pocket and dropped on the ground with a thud. It bounced once and rolled toward a corner. Carnahan stared at it. "Where did you get that?"

Mai Mai, suddenly seized by fear, was dumbfounded for a moment.

"That's a gold coin—a five-dollar piece. Where did you get it?"

"Gentleman give it to me," she said.

"What gentleman?"

"Mr. King and Mr. Gordon."

"When?"

"On the ship."

"That's almost a month ago," Carnahan said, his eyes narrowing. "Why did they give you a five-dollar gold piece?"

"Nothing."

"You're lying! They know you're a girl, don't they?"

She could feel Mr. Carnahan's hand trembling with rage. Was he jealous? She wanted him to be jealous. But she couldn't lie to him; she couldn't hide anything from him, even though Mr. King's knife flashed in her mind. "Please no tell, Mr. Carnahan," she said. "Mr. King angry if you tell. He kill me if you tell."

With a great deal of difficulty, Mai Mai stammered out the story of Toy Sing's body, the gold coin and Mr. King's threat. "Please not tell, Mr. Carnahan," she begged. "Mr. King angry if you tell. He kill Longevity and me if you tell."

Carnahan rubbed his chin pensively, his eyes narrowing in quiet anger. "I won't tell," he finally said. "All right, pick up the coin. It takes a lot of digging to make that much money."

"I go now?"

"Get out."

When Mai Mai left the cabin she was confused. What was going on in Mr. Carnahan's mind. Was he going to tell? She began to worry.

As she was trying to force Mr. Carnahan out of her mind, she saw a figure running toward her. At first she couldn't tell who it was, but when the figure grew larger she knew it was Mr. Quon. Only Mr. Quon limped like that. She stood still and waited, wondering what had happened. She had never seen Mr. Quon run before. Something important must have happened.

When Mr. Quon came closer he was panting and perspiring. "Boy, go tell Mr. Carnahan I was robbed," he shouted. "Tell him the Ringo boys did it. They took the gold, the mule, everything. Run, boy. You're faster than I am. We still have time to catch the robbers."

16

When Mai Mai arrived at the cabin, Mr. Carnahan, Mr. King and Mr. Gordon were talking at the door. Mr. Gordon was still on horseback. "What's the matter, boy?" Mr. Carnahan asked, surprised to see her. "You look like you've been kicked by a mule."

"Robber, Mr. Carnahan," Mai Mai said breathlessly.

"What?" Mr. King said, rushing into the cabin to see what had been stolen.

"Mr. Quon robbed, Mr. Carnahan. He come now."

In the distance Mr. Quon was seen limping toward the cabin. Mr. Carnahan leaped onto his horse and galloped to meet him. Mr. Gordon, who had not dismounted, followed. Mr. King came out of the cabin, checking his gun. He leaped up on his horse and joined them.

Mai Mai waited in front of the cabin, still panting from running. She saw the three men stop abruptly, their horses kicking up dust. Mr. Quon spoke to them briefly and they galloped away in the direction Mr. Quon had pointed.

When Mr. Quon arrived at the cabin his face was pale and his clothes wet and covered with dust. He sank on the nearest bench, exhausted. Mai Mai quickly poured a cup of coffee for him.

"Tea, Straw Sandal," Mr. Quon said. "The leaves are in that tin can. Thirty-five years in this country and I still haven't learned how to drink coffee. Make it strong."

Mai Mai made the tea. "Wish I had some Chinese fire liquor," Mr. Quon went on. "We are pigtail over heels in trouble now. The worst gang in the gold country—the Ringo boys."

"We killed two of them yesterday."

"That's why they robbed me. Revenge. From now on we'll be their favorite targets."

"Did you see their leader, Mr. Quon?"

"They were all dressed alike—handkerchief over their faces, dirty clothes, dirty beard, dark bandannas. But I know Ringo; I could identify him even if he were chopped into pieces. Does any of you know how to shoot?"

"Longevity can."

"That twelve-year-old boy?"

"Mr. Carnahan has just taught him how."

"Are there others who can use a gun?"

"I don't think so. Longevity said his father can use a spear."

"Spear! We'll borrow it when we roast chickens."

"But Longevity can shoot, Mr. Quon. And I can try."

Mr. Quon pointed a long fingernail at Mai Mai and said seriously, "Listen, you're only two boys. Don't ever bring a gun to the camp. If you do, it will be a good excuse for Ringo's gang to start a massacre. Tell everybody to bury his valuables. If the Ringo gang comes to bother you, don't do anything. Don't say a word. If anyone strikes you, don't strike back."

He took a sip of tea and went on, "Now go tell the villagers what I said. Be sure to hide all the valuables, and not to antagonize any of them. Just remember, they are horse thieves, stagecoach robbers, and killers."

When Mai Mai returned to the camp the villagers had already finished dinner. The news of the robbery first stunned them, then worried them. Would the Ringo gang invade the camp? If they did, would Mr. Carnahan pay for the loss? A few believed that the hanging had brought evil spirits to the camp and that everybody should prepare for the worst.

Old Wong did not know what to do with the few pieces of silver he had brought. Ta Ming suggested that he bury them immediately. Split-lip Lee worried about his old jade, a good-luck piece handed down from his ancestors. Catfish Cheong said if it was a good-luck piece, why should he worry?

Chopstick Lew disappeared for a while and everybody knew that he had gone to bury something. Mr. Ling said he would hate to lose his silk ceremonial gown. Four-eyed Dog said not to worry; if he were a foreign robber he would never touch anyone's mildew-smelling old gown, which at best was only good enough for making women's foot-binding cloth, but he wasn't sure if foreign women bound their feet. Mr. Ling, taking offense, ignored him. He dug out his Buddhist beads, counted them and murmured a prayer.

Split-lip Lee told Catfish Cheong that if he had nothing to lose, would he please stop that silly happy smile. Catfish spat and said that if Split-lip still worried about his good-luck jade piece, he could swallow it.

Mai Mai saw the villagers from the other tents hurrying in and out, hiding their valuables in the hills. Presently the conversation was switched to the wisdom of nonresistance. Four-eyed Dog opposed nonresistance. He swore that if any foreign robber touched his sacred pigtail, he would kill him. Since nobody believed that he was that brave, they didn't bother to discourage him, except Old Wong, who made the remark that all good dogs bite, naturally.

The air was tense. Mai Mai noticed that the color of Ta Ming's face was a shade lighter. Mr. Ling's hands shook a little. Four-eyed Dog swallowed more often than usual. Even Old Wong, who gave the impression of being very brave, drummed his fingers nervously.

But nothing happened that night. The next morning

everybody rose with bloodshot eyes. Mai Mai went to work with a slight sore throat. She had spent most of the sleepless night swallowing hard, expecting the Ringo gang to swoop down on them like vultures.

When she arrived at the log cabin, she was surprised to find that Mr. Carnahan, Mr. Quon, Mr. King, and Mr. Gordon were holding an urgent conference in the outer room. They all ignored her until Mr. Carnahan ordered some coffee. Mai Mai quickly built a fire in the stove and made the coffee. She missed a great deal of what they said, but from what she understood she gathered that it had something to do with the Ringo gang.

"If they want me, that is what they are going to get," Mr. Quon said, looking very tense.

"I thought you had better sense, Quon," Mr. Carnahan said. "You are only the scapegoat. I'm their target. Let me handle this."

"John," Mr. King said, "if you can't outdraw Ringo in a gunfight, you know what's going to happen. You're going to die a legitimate death, but the rest of us are going to wind up with bullet holes in our backs. This is war, men. The only solution is to go there and kill them off first. Take them by surprise!"

"Gentlemen," Mr. Quon interrupted, "Ringo challenged me and I must answer his challenge. This is my business and I have my honor to protect."

"Honor?" Mr. Gordon said. "You talk about honor with a bunch of horse thieves?"

"Since Ringo has insisted that I falsely accused them of robbing me, I must straighten this out the way he wants it."

"Doggone it, Quon," Mr. Carnahan said with disgust, "I didn't know you were suicide-prone."

"A Chinese would rather die than lose his face," Mr. Quon said. "He loses plenty of face when he evades a challenge, even though it's a horse thief's challenge. Heaven has eyes, gentlemen. Only heaven can judge who is wrong and who is right. If I have really wronged the Ringo gang, heaven will let me know."

"Oh, rubbish!" Mr. Carnahan said. "Let's get this straight; nobody is going to have a gunfight with Ringo but me. To tell the truth, you fellows aren't good enough to fight him."

"I don't mind shooting him in the back and getting it over with," Mr. King said. "We're wasting too much time on a horse thief."

"Gentlemen, to a Chinese, losing face is more serious than losing life," Mr. Quon said. "I insist that I shall face Ringo as he has requested, at the appointed place and at the appointed time. Please say no more on this subject."

"All right, Quon," Mr. Carnahan said. "If you insist on making an appointment with death, it's your own doggone business. But my conscience won't let me stand by and watch you die like a dog. Gordon, you take a position on the left of the saloon. King, plant yourself on the other side. Both of you keep an eye on Ringo's men. I'll be somewhere behind Quon. The minute I suspect foul play, I'll put a bullet through Ringo and you boys can start shooting, too. Quon, you've accepted the challenge. You won't lose anything—not even an eyebrow, let alone face. All right, boys, that's final. I don't want to hear any more arguments or any crazy ideas. We'll be at the saloon before five and take our positions before the Ringo gang arrives. Quon, don't be on time. Let Ringo wait for you. And don't go into the saloon. Let him come out to meet you."

"I never step into a saloon unnecessarily," Quon said with a faint smile. "I'm a teetotaler."

Mai Mai listened intently and got a good idea of what had been said.

Pretending that she knew nothing of it, she carried on her daily chores as usual and gave Mr. Carnahan's boots an extra shining. Mr. Quon left first. He looked grim, his brows knitted slightly. Mr. King and Mr. Gordon cleaned their guns, practiced their draws for a while and left with their equipment.

Mr. Carnahan shut himself in his room for almost an hour. Mai Mai could hear all kinds of noises behind the door; clicking of locks, opening and closing of a squeaky chest, rustling of papers, loading of guns, scratching sounds of pen against paper, and so on. Mai Mai listened intently, trying to guess what Mr. Carnahan was doing. All the noises made Mai Mai's heart beat faster. It seemed that every move Mr. Carnahan made behind that door had something to do with the exciting coming event—a gunfight with a dangerous and notorious robber.

17

For the whole afternoon Mai Mai worried about Longevity, who had been shaking with excitement about the coming gunfight. He had spent hours practicing his draw. He had saved the six bullets which Mr. Carnahan had given him for target practice, saying that he needed them for the fight. He said if there was going to be a battle, he wanted to be in it. He wanted Mr. Carnahan to know that he was not a boy anymore, but one of his gunfighters.

He juggled his gun as he talked. Mai Mai stared at

him, wondering what to do. She wished Mr. Carnahan hadn't left so early.

"Give me the gun, Longevity," she coaxed.

"You have yours," Longevity said, loading the gun.

"Mr. Carnahan won't let you go."

"He won't find me."

"What will your father say?"

"My father is a fighter."

"I am going to ask Mr. Carnahan to stop you."

"Go find him first. Don't worry, Straw Sandal. When Mr. Carnahan finds out that I've killed two robbers and wounded six, he will shake my hand and buy me a horse."

"You have only six bullets. How can you kill two and wound so many?"

"One bullet will kill one robber and wound two. It will go through them like you string water chestnuts."

"You're talking nonsense. Give me that gun. You are not going anywhere with it."

"Stop me," Longevity said. He flung the door open and dashed out with the gun. Mai Mai ran after him but Longevity had turned the corner and disappeared.

Troubled and anxious, Mai Mai took one of Mr. Carnahan's revolvers and left the cabin early. She went to the square, hid herself behind an oak tree and watched the saloon. The sun was still high. Some miners, covered with dust and looking tired, were returning from their claims. The area in front of the two taller buildings began to come to life, with people drifting into the saloon and the general store, talking and spitting tobacco juice.

She first looked for Longevity. She went from one

oak tree to another, but was unable to find him. She didn't see any familiar face until she came close to the saloon, when suddenly she saw Mr. Gordon leaning against the wall beside the saloon door. He was resting on one leg, glancing around and chewing a straw. Presently Mr. King came out of the saloon, spoke to Mr. Gordon briefly and went to the other side of the door.

Mr. King sauntered to the corner of the building, looking around as he went, turned around the corner and stopped. He leaned against the wall on the eastern side, put a foot on an oak tree stump, pushed his hat slightly to the back of his head and lighted a cigar. He watched the people drifting into the saloon as he smoked.

Mai Mai watched the two men for a moment, wondering if Ringo and his gang had arrived. She wished she could go into the saloon without being noticed. She wondered what it looked like inside.

Suddenly a hand grabbed her from behind. It was Mr. Carnahan. "What are you doing here?"

"I . . . I come to watch."

"So you eavesdropped, eh? You have no business here."

"I go look for Longevity."

"What's this bulge here?" Mr. Carnahan reached for the gun inside Mai Mai's blouse. "What is this for?"

"Maybe I help."

"You fool!" Mr. Carnahan said angrily, taking the gun away from her. "Go home. Go back to camp. Do you want to get killed?"

"I go look for Longevity," she said, starting to go.

"Go back to camp! You heard me."

As Mai Mai went to another tree, Carnahan grabbed her, lifted her up to his horse, climbed on behind her and galloped away.

For almost ten minutes Mai Mai felt the warmth of Mr. Carnahan's body and whistling wind brushing past her ears. She had never ridden anything so fast and so bumpy, with trees and brush flying past her, her bones almost shaken loose. She wondered where Mr. Carnahan was taking her. She prayed it wasn't the camp. It was so exciting to be seized like this, and taken away on a fast horse, destination unknown.

Carnahan slowed the horse and turned into a small trail leading to a mountain stream in the oak forest. When they reached the stream, he dismounted, lifted her off the horse, dumped her onto a patch of sand.

"Stay here," he commanded. "I'll come to pick you up later. If I don't find you here, I'll cut your pigtail off when I do."

He mounted his horse and was gone.

Mai Mai lay back on the sand and stared at the deep blue sky for a moment, thinking about Mr. Carnahan. Suddenly she remembered the gunfight and snapped herself out of her thoughts about a man whom she wondered if she loved.

She jumped up and started to run. When she reached the square, the sun had already fallen behind the distant mountains. Nothing had changed. Mr. Gordon was still there, chewing a straw. Mr. King, his shoulder leaning against the wall, was still glancing at the entrance to the saloon, waiting. She looked for Longevity and Mr. Carnahan but didn't see either of them. She wondered if Ringo's gang had arrived. She wished they had. She would like to see them go into the saloon with Ringo in the lead. She had visualized Ringo as a big, muscular man with a ferocious beard and bushy eyebrows and a red hooked nose with a knife scar cutting across it. She did not know why but a famous robber should look like that. She would be disappointed if he looked different.

Watching intently, her heart pounding, she counted the men going into the saloon and studied every face. She moved behind a tree about fifty yards away from the saloon for a better view. Now she could see their features and even tell the color of their faces and beards. To her disappointment nobody looked fierce enough to be a robber and nobody went in with a gang behind him.

Then she looked for Mr. Quon, hoping that if she saw him she would find Mr. Carnahan. But the skinny Mr. Quon did not appear until almost twenty minutes later. He was dressed in a yellow silk gown with a sash tied around his waist. He wore a pair of satin shoes with white soles, like those worn by rich men in China. He walked slowly toward the saloon.

About thirty yards from the buiding, he halted. A man with a large hat who had been sauntering in front of the door suddenly darted into the saloon. Both Mr. Gordon and Mr. King became alert. They were now facing Mr. Quon. Mr. Gordon spat out the straw that he had been chewing for a long time.

Mai Mai searched for Mr. Carnahan, but he was

still nowhere in sight. The street looked normal. Miners in red shirts were coming and going. A few drifted into the saloon, unsuspecting.

Presently the man with the large hat darted out again. "C'mon in, Quon," he yelled. "What are you standing there for? Afraid?"

"Tell Mr. Ringo to come out," Mr. Quon said quietly. "I am meeting him here."

The exchange of words almost electrified the street. People turned. Some came closer to the saloon. Others took cover behind oak trees. A few hurried into the general store. Everybody seemed to know what was going to happen. The air became so tense that even the birds in the oak trees seemed to have become quiet.

Mai Mai watched the saloon door, her hands wet and her heart pounding against her ribs. Suddenly the swinging door burst open and a medium-sized man, wearing a black hat slightly to one side, stepped out. He was about thirty-five. He had deep-set dark eyes, thin eyebrows and a flat nose. His mustache was neatly trimmed. He was impressively armed with two guns that dangled from his sides over his tight pants. Tucked in his ammunition belt was a large bowie knife. His brownish sheepskin jacket, old and weatherbeaten, fitted well on his lean body. He walked with his hands spread out slightly, his dusty brownish boots squeaking. About twenty feet away from Quon he stopped.

"Where is your gun, Quon?" he asked, his voice metallic and cold.

Quon stood staring at him, looking small and frail.

"Do you hear me, Quon?" Ringo asked again. "I said where is your gun?"

"Shoot, Mr. Ringo," Quon said quietly.

"I'm not going to shoot you like a dog. Somebody give him a gun."

The man with the large hat took off his gunbelt and went to Quon. "Wear this, Quon, like a good boy," he said.

There was some laughter from the bystanders. Mai Mai looked and found a lot more people gathering. They stood at a safe distance from either Quon or Ringo. Mr. King was still standing beside the wall, glancing to his right and left. Mr. Gordon had moved farther away from the saloon door, watching a group of bystanders. Mr. Carnahan was still nowhere to be seen.

"Take this, Quon," the man with the large hat said, dangling his gunbelt in front of him. "If you don't take it I'm going to grab your silly pigtail and give you a good spanking."

There was more laughter. Mr. Quon stared at him, his face pale with anger. He made no move to accept the gun.

"Show him the gun is loaded," Ringo said.

"Oh, a coward, eh?" the man with the large hat said, grinning. He took the gun out of its holster, flipped the revolver open and showed Mr. Quon the bullets. "Six bullets, every one of 'em capable of drilling holes in a Chinaman's thick skull!"

Pleased with himself, the man laughed. Mr. Quon took a deep breath as if to control himself. Suddenly he smiled and accepted the gun belt with a slight bow.

"That's the boy," the man said, backing away.

Mr. Quon put on the gunbelt carefully, his eyes on

Ringo. After he had buckled the belt he put his hands down, like a gunfighter. But his clothes, his pigtail and his cap with the red little button on top presented a peculiar sight in the middle of the street. A few people shouted funny remarks. A few others laughed. Most of the onlookers watched him tensely. Ringo took another step forward, his fingers working.

Suddenly Ringo's hand went for his gun. Almost instantly there was a crack, like the explosion of a small firecracker. The laughter and loud talk stopped abruptly. There was a moment of deadly silence. Ringo dropped his gun and slumped to the ground. Mr. Quon had shot him with a Deringer that he had drawn from his large sleeve. Hardly had he returned the Deringer to his sleeve than there was another shot, a louder explosion ringing through the air. A man about twenty yards behind Mr. Quon staggered and fell on his face, his gun falling from his hand. Then there was a succession of gunshots and two more men fell. Mr. Quon dropped to the ground as if he had been hit, too.

As if from nowhere, Mr. Carnahan appeared. Cautiously he walked toward Mr. Quon, a gun in each hand. From the other side of the street, both Mr. King and Mr. Gordon, their guns drawn, were backing away from the saloon and sidling toward Mr. Carnahan. Mr. Quon stood up and dusted his silk gown.

"Listen, Ringo's men," Mr. Carnahan said, "I give you an hour to get out of town quietly. This place is only for respectable miners. You undesirables and horse thieves have no business here. If I find any of you still in Hangtown after dusk, you'll be as dead as Ringo here. And if any of you dare to level a gun at Mr.

Quon's back again, you will—let me borrow a Chinese phrase—join your ancestors pronto!"

"Thank you, Mr. Carnahan," Mr. Quon said with a faint smile.

"That's all," Mr. Carnahan shouted to the crowd. "And let me warn you again. I'm going into that saloon for a drink. When I come out of that door, you'd better be gone. Don't make me use my guns again tonight!" When he finished, he turned to Mr. Quon and said, "Let's all go in and have a drink."

"I'm a teetotaler," Quon said, "but I need one now." He took off the gunbelt and tossed it away as though it were something dirty.

"Hey, you there, boy!" Mr. Carnahan shouted at Mai Mai, who was still hiding behind the oak tree. "You might as well come too."

Mai Mai, surprised that Mr. Carnahan had seen her, came out from behind the oak tree sheepishly. "C'mon, boy," Mr. Carnahan said. "You want to see what a saloon looks like, don't you?"

"Yes, sir," Mai Mai said, glad that Longevity had not shown up—glad that everything was over.

As she followed Mr. Carnahan eagerly toward the saloon, she saw seven or eight men mount their horses and gallop away. The man with the large hat picked up the gunbelt that Mr. Quon had tossed away, leaped on his horse and followed. Mr. King and Mr. Gordon, their hands on their guns, watched them until they disappeared in a big cloud of dust.

At the door of the saloon Mr. Quon said, "I can really take care of myself, Mr. Carnahan."

"You can take care of yourself, all right," Mr. Carnahan said. "I don't think any gunfighter in California can outdraw you. That goes for me, too. But you don't have eyes in the back of your head. By the way, that's quite a draw. How did you do it?"

"It's easy," Quon said, leveling his right arm. With lightening speed the Deringer darted out of his sleeve.

"Doggone it! Faster than a snake's tongue," Carnahan said.

"It's called 'snake tongue draw,'" Mr. Quon said. "But you must wear a Chinese gown with a large sleeve to take full advantage of it."

"You inscrutable Oriental," Mr. Carnahan said, heading for the bar with a smile.

Mai Mai, deeply impressed, followed Mr. Quon closely. She was proud of him. She must tell Longevity about his "snake tongue draw."

18

✿ Longevity had run into Ta Ming when he left the cabin, and now he was unhappy because his father had forbidden him to join in the gunfight. It was not until Mai Mai had told him all about it that he came to life again. For the whole evening he wouldn't talk about anything else. When he asked questions, one after another, Mai Mai couldn't resist the temptation to add a few legs to the snake.

As they talked in the tent, the others pretended that they were not interested. But the next day when word went around that the robbers had been buried behind the saloon, the coolies avoided looking in that direction for fear they might catch the attention of evil spirits.

Mai Mai performed her daily chores as usual. But she didn't have a chance to be alone with Mr. Carnahan again. Since the gunfight he came and went with Mr. King and Mr. Gordon. He still called her "boy" and ignored her most of the time.

Pay day was finally approaching. Everybody at the camp counted the days on his fingers. The discussion of future plans was resumed with great enthusiasm. Even Mr. Ling became less aloof and participated in conversations without being particular about the subject matter. Quite a few others who rarely talked to anyone had also come to life, their dull eyes beginning to sparkle.

Four-eyed Dog burned some extra incense; he did not want any evil spirits wandering around the tent on pay day. Old Wong took out his silk gown and smoothed the wrinkles with a dampened hand, readying it to wear on pay day. Chopstick Lew plucked and trimmed his thin mustache and rebraided his sacred queue. He sniffed at his smelling jar full of sandalwood dust occasionally, wrinkling his nose and twisting his upper lip before sneezing. More people sneezed as pay day came closer, as nasal explosions, like firecrackers, were festive; they were also a good sign, indicating longevity. Every time someone sneezed somebody else would say, "Happy long life."

Ta Ming was the only man who did not reveal his future plans. Sometimes he squatted under a tree, smoking a bamboo pipe, lost in deep thought. Mai Mai wondered what he was thinking about. A woman? A second wife? "Look at his eyes," she said to Longevity one evening. "They are dreamy. That smile cannot fool anybody."

"He talks a lot about repairing and beautifying the ancestral burial grounds," Longevity said. "That is what he is thinking about."

"That is only a cover-up," Mai Mai said. "He is too young to think of going to the other world, Longevity. A handsome man should think of marriage and children. Five sons are the minimum number a man should have."

"How many do you want?"

"I want a dozen. If I can find the right man."

"Man?"

"I mean woman." She laughed. "When I'm excited I don't know whether I'm talking about a cat's paw or a donkey's hind leg."

"You're blushing."

"I'm excited."

"Why are you so excited?"

"Doesn't gold excite you, Longevity?" Her cheeks burned and she quickly changed the subject.

Pay day came. Everybody returned to the tent early, changed into clean clothes and waited. Four-eyed Dog's Adam's apple went up and down, but he feigned calmness like the others.

Longevity made tea and served it. Both Split-lip Lee and Old Wong drummed on their teacups without drinking the tea. Chopstick Lew puffed on his bamboo pipe vigorously although it had no tobacco in it. Ta Ming sat on a little wooden stool and tapped the ground with a foot restlessly. Catfish Cheong kept clearing his throat as if he were about to make a speech. They all tried to look casual, grinning a little. And for the first time they sat together without talking.

Before dusk Mr. Quon arrived with the gold in a canvas bag. He had divided the gold into equal shares, neatly wrapped in oil paper. Everybody accepted his parcel with studied calmness, swallowing hard, hands trembling a little. Mai Mai, to her surprise, received two five-dollar gold coins for her service at the cabin.

When Mr. Quon gave Ta Ming his parcel he said that Mr. Carnahan had decided to pay him the full ten percent, as Longevity had proved to be a useful boy. The company would pay for his keep; it might even pay him a salary when he was a year or two older and learned to do some kitchen work, such as helping to bake bread.

Everybody waited for Ta Ming to open his parcel first. Ta Ming opened it with a gratified smile. But when he took a look at the contents, his face fell. The others opened theirs. All frowned. Mr. Quon grinned with embarrassment. He gave a little speech. Next month they would have better luck. The first month was always poor, as nobody was experienced. Besides, food was expensive in the gold country. After expenses, his own share did not come to more than an ounce either. And he was a part owner of the mine.

Catfish Cheong was the first one to grumble audibly. Split-lip Lee calculated something on his fingers with great concentration, mumbling numbers. Chopstick Lew started groaning as though his old ailment had returned.

Suddenly there was a lot of complaining and grumbling.

Mr. Quon waved both his hands in the air. "Fellow countrymen," he called, "listen to me for a moment. This is only the beginning. We did not have much luck with these claims. We will soon move to new claims upriver. We will dig deeper and use cradles. We might even have a good strike. If we make a real strike, there will be no more digging, no more washing. We will just bend down and pick up gold nuggets as big as goose eggs. Some miners upriver have already done just that!"

"I won't be that lucky," Old Wong said.

"Luck knocks on the door of anybody," Mr. Quon said. "But we must open the door to receive it. I was a gambler once. I know what I am talking about."

"How to open the door? You tell me!" Four-eyed Dog shouted.

"By working hard, by taking a chance, by facing adversity with courage!"

"If the door is that hard to open," Four-eyed Dog said to nobody in particular, "I'll leap out the window to meet Mr. Luck." He was disappointed that nobody laughed at his joke.

Split-lip Lee finished his calculation. He had reached the conclusion that at this rate of earning it would take him a hundred and fifty years to buy an acre of rice field, and another fifty years to pay for a modest wedding. By that time, he added, he would be a little too old to take a wife.

Ta Ming rose and made a proposal. The Chinese would continue to work hard, but to receive a basic monthly pay of fifty dollars, plus a bonus. If everybody agreed, perhaps Mr. Quon could bring it up with Mr. Carnahan.

Everybody nodded and grumbled his approval. Mr. Quon tried to argue, but the coolies were firm. Coughing loudly he left the camp.

Ta Ming called a meeting of all the Chinese. They all agreed to the proposal and elected Ta Ming to write it. They would put their seals on it.

Using a crate as a table Ta Ming composed the proposal as best he could with black ink and brush. All the others waited outside, their seals ready.

The proposal was a lengthy document written in classical Chinese. Ta Ming read it aloud, his head shaking rhythmically in a scholarly fashion. Everybody was impressed except Mr. Ling, who disapproved of the style, the wrong use of many words and the misquotes of Confucius. But the coolies ignored him and put their seals on it eagerly. Those who did not have a seal used their right thumbs.

Mai Mai was happy with her shining gold coins, which most of the coolies eyed with envy. With three five-dollar gold pieces in her pocket she felt like the richest Chinese at the camp.

The next morning she went to work early. When she arrived she heard voices behind the door of Mr. Carnahan's room. Mr. Quon came out first. She greeted him but Mr. Quon only grunted and left in a hurry.

She tidied up the outer room as the conference continued in Mr. Carnahan's room. She could hear voices clearly but had no idea what they were talking about.

Suddenly Mr. King said, "That damned boy!"

"You don't really mean to harm that boy, do you, King?" Mr. Carnahan said.

"So far he hasn't told the others, has he?" Mr. King asked.

"I don't think so. This proposal has nothing to do with it. The Chinese are just unhappy about the ten percent. We did not cheat them. This is what they have earned on a ten percent basis. The expenses are high and the diggings are poor."

"I still think we ought to tell them to go to hell," Mr. Gordon said. "They signed an indenture on such terms, didn't they?"

"Fair play should be considered," Mr. Carnahan said. "We are not dealing with a bunch of animals. Even animals deserve some consideration."

"You can't make a mule move unless you give it a kick in the right place," Mr. King said.

"A kick will make a mule go, yes," Mr. Carnahan said. "But a mule also kicks back."

"That's what you are afraid of, John?" Mr. King asked.

"I'm thinking of fairness. The way you dumped that body in the river is unfair enough. I've been feeling uncomfortable about it ever since I found out."

"That damned boy!" Mr. King mumbled angrily. "I should have cut his throat."

"Listen, King," Mr. Carnahan said, "it's not his fault that he talked. I accused him of stealing the five-dollar gold piece. He was so scared that he had to tell the truth. Let's forget about the boy, understand?"

"Just make sure he doesn't tell the others, or we've got another headache coming."

"You just make sure you don't do it again, King," Carnahan said. "I don't like it."

"What are you talking about?"

"Dumping corpses into the river. They want to be buried in their villages beside their families. That's their religion. Let's stick to the agreement."

"We've been losing money on this mine, John. We don't have the cash to spare. A corpse rots anywhere, whether it's in this country or in China. It saves time and money to feed it to the fish."

"Listen, King," Mr. Carnahan said firmly, "the Chinese believe in joining their ancestors after death. To them the custom is sacred. I said let's stick to the agreement."

"All right, John. You're the brains. I won't argue. I just hope no more Chinamen die. What are you going to do about their demands?"

"I'll think it over."

"Don't forget. We've been losing money."

"It was a gamble from the start. We understood that."

"Let them know the food is expensive," Mr. Gordon said. "Eggs cost a dollar apiece in this damned place. They ought to be grateful that they are well fed."

"We never feed them eggs," Mr. Carnahan said. "We have plenty of rice and cheap ham. That's all, boys. I'll meet you at the mine. Let's see if our luck is better at the new claims."

Chairs were heard moving. The meeting was over. Mai Mai tensed. She quickly went to a corner and busied herself sweeping the floor.

The door opened. Mr. King and Mr. Gordon were

gone. There was nothing outside but a cloud of dust kicked up by the horses, the buzzing of flies and the warm morning sunshine.

Then the door to Mr. Carnahan's room opened again. Mai Mai's heart jumped. Carnahan came out; he stopped at the door for a brief moment, staring at her. She wanted to run, but her feet disobeyed her. He came to her, took her by her shoulders and smiled. Then he kissed her gently on the mouth.

19

✿ The six new claims were about two miles upriver from the old one, which Mr. Carnahan abandoned without regret. The Chinese established a new camp closer to the mines. They pitched their tents at the foot of a hill that resembled a dragon's head. According to Mr. Ling, everybody was now living on the dragon's spine and nobody should have any more fear of evil spirits. Many made food offerings and burned incense for the dragon. Mr. Quon now visited the camp and the mines on horseback. Mr. Carnahan had great hopes for the new mines. He installed two cradles beside the river and bought a wind machine to separate the gold from the black sand.

Six men were assigned to handle each cradle—two shovelling earth, two pouring water and two rocking them. The cradles indeed proved more labor-saving. The men operated them efficiently without practicing.

The job for the rest of the Chinese was simple—digging and carrying the dirt to the river. The mines were in the hills about half a mile north of the river. Because of the distance, the Chinese used their own carrying method—balancing two loaded pails on their shoulders on a pole, swinging them as they trotted toward the river.

For three days after they had moved, they worked hard, wondering if Mr. Carnahan would grant them their demand for a salary. On the fourth day there was still no word from Mr. Carnahan. When questioned, Mr. Quon would only evade the issue.

Ta Ming asked the villagers to be patient. It was not until the end of the week that Mr. Quon came with the good news. Mr. Carnahan had agreed to pay every worker, regardless of job, three ounces of gold a month, plus a bonus, which would be five percent of the net profit. Mr. Quon said that was almost forty-five dollars a month, not counting the bonus.

The Chinese held a meeting and considered the offer fair. At dinnertime everybody was in a festive mood. Mr. Ling changed into his old ceremonial gown. Old Wong served a little wine, which he had fermented from leftover rice. Four-eyed Dog entertained everybody with a folk song that frightened away the birds in the nearby trees. Everybody was happy and worked twice as hard at the mines the next day.

In the meantime Mr. Carnahan passed the word around that he was thinking about increasing the yield further by introducing another machine called a sluice, an open trough about fourteen feet long and two feet wide. It had wide slats at the bottom called riffles. Pay dirt and water would be put in at one end and as it sloshed through the sluice, the gold would drop to the bottom and be caught by the riffles.

He was as good as his word. Presently two sluices were installed. They proved to be very satisfactory. Again Mr. Carnahan spread the word that he had even bigger things in mind, such as a real strike. Mr. Quon said that in order to make a strike, the miners must go deeper—perhaps twenty feet. He told a few stories about recent strikes in the neighborhood. One miner working with his brother made the biggest strike up-river. For ten days they dug out nothing but pure gold nuggets as big as goose eggs. They made twenty thousand dollars apiece. But Mr. Quon did not neglect to state the fact that it was a gamble.

Immediately after Mr. Quon had told the story, Split-lip Lee started calculating five percent of twenty thousand dollars on his fingers. When he came up with the impressive total of one thousand dollars, he was all smiles and for a long time he did not stop rolling his eyes.

When this story was circulated, the Chinese were all willing to go deep to make a strike. It was the only chance to become wealthy. Again they elected Ta Ming to talk to Mr. Quon, expressing their mutual desire to gamble.

Finally Mr. Carnahan announced that he had decided to gamble by going deeper. Through Mr. Quon he warned that the work would be harder and the cost heavier. He asked the Chinese not to change their minds in the middle of the job.

The Chinese agreed. Catfish Cheong rubbed his hands eagerly, saying that he was ready to go a hundred feet deep if necessary. Old Wong remarked that going a hundred feet underground might reach the eighteenth level of hell, where the ghost king Yan Wong resided. Twenty feet deep was all he was willing to go. Four-eyed Dog considered mention of the ghost king highly unnecessary. It would bring bad luck, he said, and he quickly burned three sticks of incense.

Chopstick Lew thought the whole project was impossible. He had never seen a ladder more than fifteen feet long. Besides, carrying pay dirt up a ladder was a feat only an acrobat could accomplish. He couldn't do it himself because he suffered dizzy spells. He asked for other assignments.

Ta Ming reminded him that he might carry up nothing but gold nuggets as big as goose eggs. Chopsticks thought it over and corrected his original statement, saying that he only suffered dizzy spells occasionally.

From that night on, the Chinese talked about nothing but gold nuggets. It took Mr. Carnahan three days to get everything ready for deep mining. He bought lumber, long sturdy ropes and large wooden buckets.

The men in each tent were divided into two working

groups. One did the digging and the other hoisted up pay dirt with ropes and buckets. They switched the work every other day, and when they reached the depth of twenty feet, they were to ask Mr. Carnahan to come down to analyze the formation of dirt. Mr. Carnahan would decide whether to go deeper or to go sideways. If they went sideways, they would build a door with lumber to support the weight, then dig a tunnel following the vein.

For a month the Chinese worked hard at the new mines. Day and night they prayed for a strike. Four-eyed Dog kept talking about a strike, and he had never before enjoyed so much attention.

But nobody made a strike. At the end of the month a faint feeling of futility began to invade the camp. The bonus was negligible. Old Wong declared that at this rate of earning nobody could become wealthy until he was three hundred years old.

Mai Mai enjoyed working for Mr. Carnahan, cooking his meals and washing his clothes. She wondered if Mr. Carnahan loved her. He had never said the word "love," although his kisses had said a great deal. Would a few tender words from Mr. Carnahan's heart fulfill her wishes completely? She often felt as though she had been watching a delightful Chinese opera with the actors singing and dancing in a beautiful pageant without sound; she could see their mouths move yet could not hear the songs and the words.

One evening, while walking back to the tent from the cabin, Mai Mai heard hooves behind her. She turned and found Mr. King catching up with her on horseback.

He stopped and told her to climb aboard. He was on his way to the Chinese camp. Mai Mai hesitated. Mr. King reached down and pulled her up onto the horse. She smelled his heavy whiskey breath and tried to leap off, but he tightened his grip around her waist.

The horse turned toward the hills, struggled uphill and into the woods. She decided it was foolish to struggle. It would be better to submit to him than to die in the wilderness with her throat cut.

Mr. King dismounted and tied his horse to a large pine tree. It was a nice secluded spot on a slope, surrounded by pines and bushes and rocks. The small trail leading downhill was almost covered by weeds. Down below was Hangtown, to the east the Chinese camp and the river. If she shrieked loudly enough somebody in Hangtown might hear her. But she was not so stupid as to try that.

"Get down," Mr. King ordered, unholstering his revolver. Holding the gun in one hand he unbuckled his gunbelt, his red eyes smiling. She could almost feel them. She felt a sudden revulsion, but kept quiet.

"I said to get down," he commanded again, his voice impatient.

Mai Mai obeyed. By now Mr. King had tossed his gunbelt and bowie knife on the ground.

"You sure fooled me," he said, "with Carnahan calling you 'boy' and all that. You're not bad looking, inspite of your pigtail and the dirt on your face."

He grabbed her and she bit his hand. *"Ouch!"* he yelled, letting her go.

Mai Mai ran all the way down the trail to Hang,

town. She burst into Carnahan's cabin, her blouse torn, hands and feet bleeding. Carnahan stared at her in disbelief. "What happened?"

Mai Mai breathlessly told him. Carnahan's eyes narrowed. He rushed into his room, and a moment later he came out wearing his gunbelt. "You wait here," he commanded.

Mai Mai watched him mount his horse. "What if he gets killed?" The thought horrified her. She dashed out of the cabin to stop him, but Carnahan had already reined his horse to an abrupt stop. He had seen King coming.

He returned to the cabin, his nervous horse leaping and snorting. As he dismounted and tied it, King arrived. King greeted him as though nothing had happened. Carnahan stood in front of the cabin, his hands down, his jawbones working. King hitched his horse and walked toward the cabin. "Well, John," he said pleasantly, "didn't expect you back so early."

When he reached the cabin, Carnahan hit him. The blow sent King tumbling and falling on his haunches. King looked at Carnahan, surprised, feeling his jaw. A trickle of blood appeared at the corner of his mouth. He wiped it. "So the no-good girl is back," he said. "Look, John—"

Before he finished, Carnahan grabbed him, pulled him up and hit him again. King shook his head clear on the dusty ground. Suddenly he reached for his gun. Carnahan kicked it away. King grimaced. Carnahan took King's bowie knife and tossed it away, then backed up, waiting. "Get up," he said.

Mai Mai withdrew to the cabin, unable to watch

anymore. King got up, wiped the blood from his mouth, grinning. "Look, John," he said, advancing, "I don't know what that China doll told you, but it was a misunderstanding, I tell you. We are friends and partners. Let's not let a Chinese coolie girl——"

Carnahan swung again. King ducked and swung back. Mai Mai, standing with her back against the wall of the cabin, avoided looking out. She heard the blows clearly; they sounded like firecrackers. Every cracking sound made her heart jump. She did not know how long they fought. An occasional groan told her someone was hurt. She hated death; she hated fights, or even quarrels. She regretted that she had come to the cabin. She should have gone to the camp instead, and kept the whole thing a secret. No matter if Mr. Carnahan won or lost, King was going to kill him, and perhaps kill her, too. Perhaps it would be safer for him if she left the camp and Hangtown.

The firecrackers stopped. She was still afraid to look. She waited, holding her breath, her hands over her face, her heart thumping, knowing that the first one to enter the cabin would be the winner. But for a long time nobody entered.

She couldn't stand the suspense any longer. She went to the door to look, her fingers pulling at her lower teeth, her lips trembling.

Carnahan, bloody and breathless, stood over King and spoke for the first time since the fight had started, "Keep your hands off that girl, understand? I'm thinking of marrying her." Then, dusting off his red shirt, he staggered toward the cabin.

20

For two days Longevity wondered why Straw Sandal looked so worried. In fact, everybody at the Chinese camp seemed to worry about something. He was the only one who had no worries. And he was happy about his progress in shooting and juggling the gun. Now he could easily hit any branch on the oak tree at a distance of fifty yards, and he had dug out a deep hole in the tree trunk by scoring many bull's eyes there. "Now it is time to learn Mr. Quon's sleeve trick," he told himself. Every time he thought of Straw Sandal's description of Mr. Quon's "snake tongue draw" his heart pounded with excitement.

It was early afternoon. After shooting practice, he juggled his gun for an hour under the oak tree. When he returned the gun to the cabin he was surprised to find Mai Mai gone and the cabin untidy. He washed the cups and put things in order. The sun was warm. He did not want to go back to the empty camp. He went back to the tree at the square, sat in the shade and day-dreamed. He dreamed of the day he would ride into the camp shooting and juggling the gun and dismounting like Mr. Carnahan, with his energetic horse snorting, leaping on its hind legs and kicking up dust. Four-eyed Dog would stare at him and gape in admiration. His father would smile proudly, and announce that from now on his son would be the official protector of the Chinese camp. . . .

Suddenly he saw Mr. Quon ride through Hangtown on his way to the Chinese camp. He rose quickly and caught up with him and greeted him pleasantly. "What are you doing here, Longevity?" Mr. Quon asked.

"I just finished working in Mr. Carnahan's cabin."

"Climb up. You might as well save some walking. It's a hot day."

Mr. Quon reined the horse to a stop. Longevity scrambled up behind him. They rode quietly for a while. Longevity's heart thumped more violently now; he was trying to work up his courage to ask Mr. Quon a great favor.

It was not until they had almost reached the Chinese camp that he finally stammered out his wish.

"Why do you want to learn that, Longevity?" Mr.

Quon asked. "Shooting is like a two-edged sword. You protect yourself with it and you also invite danger because of it. A polite bow and a genuine smile are better protection anywhere."

"Mr. Carnahan said I should learn how to handle a gun," Longevity said, finding himself more bold now.

"Did he?"

"Yes. He has been teaching me. But I like your sleeve trick, Mr. Quon."

"Do you have a derringer?"

"No. But I will save money to buy one."

"Are you right-handed or left-handed?"

"Right-handed."

"Show me your right hand."

Longevity put out his right hand for Mr. Quon to look. "You have long fingers. That's good," Mr. Quon said. "Bend your wrist. See if you can touch your wrist with your own fingers."

Longevity could not. No matter how far he bent his wrist, the fingers were still an inch away from his own wrist.

"Practice every day," Mr. Quon said. "That is your first lesson. When the day comes that you can bend your wrist and pinch your own arm, you are ready to learn the sleeve trick. Like this." Mr. Quon extended his left arm and pulled up his sleeve. He bent his left wrist almost double and pinched his left arm with his long fingers. "See? You cannot learn the 'snake tongue draw' until you can do this first."

"Where do you keep your derringer, Mr. Quon?" Longevity asked.

"In my right sleeve," Mr. Quon said. "Don't ask me

to show it to you. Never show a gun to anybody. That is the first thing you must remember. Always protect yourself with your other weapons first—a bow and a smile. As I said before, the other weapons are better protection; they rarely fail. Through all my life only twice was I forced to use my derringer. I hope I shall never use it again. Do you still want to learn?"

"Yes, Mr. Quon," Longevity said eagerly. He had already started bending both his wrists busily. Now that he felt closer to Mr. Quon he ventured his next big question that he had always wanted to ask. "Do you really have a wooden leg, Mr. Quon?"

"That is no secret, Longevity," Mr. Quon said. He reached down and knocked on his leg with his knuckles. "When you can't run as fast as the next man, you learn something else to compensate for your handicap. Just like a turtle; it grows a shell to compensate for its slowness. My shell is not my derringer, understand; it is my ability to control anger. Nobody is immune to emotions, Longevity, especially anger. But you can learn to control it. It protects you as well as a turtle's shell protects the turtle."

"How did you lose your leg, Mr. Quon?"

"I thought everybody knew. It is no secret."

"Did a rattlesnake really bite it and you cut off the leg yourself with a pair of scissors?"

"What?" Mr. Quon asked. Suddenly he laughed. "That's a new one. I've heard several versions of the story. One was that I was chasing a woman and she slammed her door on my leg. The other was that I was crossing the Yangtse River in China and a crocodile snapped it off. Now a rattlesnake has taken a bite of it, ha ha! This new one wins my award for the most imaginative. A pair of scissors, ha ha ha!"

Longevity had never heard Mr. Quon laugh before. It was a funny laugh, loud and clear. It was also contagious. Longevity couldn't help but laugh too.

"Where did you hear that, Longevity?" Mr. Quon asked.

"Four-eyed Dog told me," Longevity said.

"Oh, him."

"He tells a lot of stories. My father says he smells everything a mile away."

"Well," Mr. Quon said, still laughing, "I sincerely hope he can smell gold."

"How did you really lose your leg, Mr. Quon?"

"I was walking down a hill in San Francisco, minding my own business. Suddenly I slipped and broke my leg. It became infected and had to be cut off. That's all. It's not an exciting way to lose a leg, but it is a fact. Disappointed?"

"Yes," Longevity said.

"Life is full of disappointments if you are not prepared for them," Mr. Quon said solemnly. "Most of the excitements in life exist in people's minds. Take mining for gold, for instance. I don't really expect a strike, so I will not be disappointed when we don't make a strike. It is only when you dream of a strike and the good things that go along with it that you become vulnerable. You become crushed when your dreams don't come true. But if you do make a strike, other things will disappoint you. People have the weakness to create excitement in their minds and become disappointed when they face reality. Do you understand me, Longevity?"

"No," Longevity said. He was busy thinking of Mr. Quon's snake tongue draw.

"You will," Mr. Quon said. "In a year or two."

They rode quietly for the rest of the way until they reached the first tent. It was dinnertime and usually there was activity in front of those tents—washing, cooking, carpentering. But this evening the tent was completely deserted. They rode past the first tent and found the second one empty also.

"Get down," Mr. Quon said.

Longevity quickly got off the horse. Mr. Quon dismounted, went into the tent and came out. "Where are these people?" he asked, hurrying to the third tent on foot. Longevity followed.

The third tent was also empty. Longevity ran to his own tent, the fourth. There was nobody. Nothing had been moved. His own bed was neatly made. So was his father's.

"Father," he called. "Father! Where are you?"

"Let's go to the mines," Mr. Quon said, hurrying to his horse. Longevity ran ahead of him and brought the horse to Mr. Quon. They mounted and rode toward the hills, kicking the horse with their heels to make it trot.

"They may have made a strike," Longevity said, excited.

Mr. Quon rode in silence for a moment, then spoke, "Let us pray it is a strike, Longevity. Let us pray."

Before they reached the mines, Longevity saw Straw

Sandal and all the other Chinese digging frantically at one claim. "A strike!" Longevity shouted. "It's my father's mine! We are rich!"

He kicked the horse and slapped its flank with the palm of his hand. "Hurry, hurry!" he kept shouting. "It's a strike!" The horse began to gallop laboriously, struggling uphill.

When they reached the mine, nobody paid any attention to them. Mr. King and Mr. Gordon were also there, digging. Mr. Carnahan, washed the perspiration and looking dirty for the first time, was running around shouting instructions. Mr. Quon and Longevity dismounted quickly and ran to him.

"What is it, Mr. Carnahan," Mr. Quon asked, "a strike?"

"Pick up something and start digging," Mr. Carnahan said. "This shaft collapsed. Three men are buried in it!"

Without a word Mr. Quon picked up a shovel and plunged to work. Longevity was stunned for a moment. When he realized what had happened, he made a dash for the hole. Mr. Carnahan grabbed him. Longevity struggled, trying to leap into the hole.

"Boy, boy, calm down! Your father may still be alive. Calm down!"

When Longevity became hysterical, Mr. Carnahan slapped him. "Sit down, boy," he said as Longevity began to get control of himself. "You're only obstructing the work by behaving like this. All right, men! Let's get those three poor devils. They may still be alive!"

21

By the time they dug the three men out, their bodies were already cold, their faces purple. Mr. Carnahan closed their eyes and officially pronounced Ta Ming, Four-eyed Dog, and Old Wong dead.

Mai Mai and a few other miners wept. Longevity was too shocked to cry. He returned to the tent, sat on the floor and stared at his father's empty bed dry-eyed, refusing to go to sleep. Mr. Quon came in before midnight and told him that a tent had been pitched for the three dead men and that incense had been burned for them. He also assured Longevity that arrangements would be made to return his father's body to China.

"Remember, Longevity," he said, "life is full of disappointments. A wise man always prepares for the worst."

After Mr. Quon had left, Longevity tossed in bed, unable to sleep. A horrible thought came to his mind and made him jerk up to a sitting position in a cold sweat. Were Mr. King and Mr. Gordon going to dump his father's body in the river as they had Toy Sing's?

He crawled out of the tent. Chopstick was sound asleep, snoring a little through his mouth. Mai Mai had turned away from him and was sleeping with her face buried in her arms.

Outside the half moon shone brightly among stars in the clear dark sky. A breeze rustled the leaves in the oak trees. It was a chilly night. Longevity did not know how late it was. He hoped it was not close to dawn. In China he could tell time from the barking of dogs or the crowing of a rooster, but in this foreign wilderness there was no way to tell except by the glow of the rising sun.

He could see the new tent. It had been pitched at the foot of the hill about fifty yards from his own. He hurried to it quietly, making sure that nobody saw him. At the door of the tent a few sticks of incense had just finished burning. Some villagers must have offered them when the bodies were being moved in. "I must burn some more," Longevity thought, "and burn some paper money, too."

Inside the tent the three bodies lay side by side. In

the darkness they looked like three men sleeping peacefully. Even though Ta Ming had been the tallest, Longevity could not tell at a glance who was who. He crawled from one end of the tent to the other until he identified his father's body, which lay on the right, facing the door. Suddenly he felt his throat swell. He sobbed until he remembered what he had come for.

Quickly he dragged his father's body out of the tent. The hill was steep but he knew he had to carry it up there and bury it before dawn. He tried to carry the body, but it was too heavy. "If only I can get him on my shoulder," he thought, and made several attempts to lift the body.

Then he tried to drag the body uphill. After a few yards he was exhausted. "I must get a horse," he thought. As he was pulling his father's body into the brush, he heard a crunching noise that made him jump. He waited, staring into the bushes where the noise had come from.

In the darkness he saw the top of a bush move and a head pop out. Longevity's first reaction was to run.

"Don't be afraid, Longevity," the voice said. "It is only me."

Longevity had no trouble recognizing Straw Sandal's voice. It was high pitched, almost like a woman's. "What are you doing here?" he asked.

"I could not sleep," Mai Mai said. "I came out to wash my hands."

"I came out to wash my hands too," Longevity said.

"But you are dragging something uphill. What is it?"

"Nothing."

"What is that?" Mai Mai asked, pointing to Ta Ming's body.

"You won't tell!"

"No, why should I tell?"

"I'm hiding my father's body so they won't dump it into the river."

"You need help."

"No, I don't."

"Let me help you. I am your friend, am I not?"

"I must get a horse," Longevity said. "And some incense and paper money."

"You need a pick and a spade, too, if you want to bury a body."

"I'm going to get the horse first."

"I'll get the rest," Mai Mai said. "I still have some incense. I can get paper money from Mr. Ling or Chopstick Lew."

"Don't!" Longevity almost shouted.

"They won't know. I'm going to borrow it while they are asleep. You offered to borrow some for me when my brother died, remember? Go get the horse. We're wasting precious time standing here talking."

Longevity pulled the body into the brush and started for Hangtown hurriedly. He decided to bury his father's body on the other side of the hill so nobody would find it. Only a horse could carry the body over the hill before sunrise. The thought of dawn became more threatening every minute. He quickened his steps, then began to run.

He was familiar with all Mr. Carnahan's horses, but he had no time to choose. He took the first one, patted its neck to soothe it, and quietly guided it away from the log cabin. The street was deserted and looked ghostly in the darkness.

The moment he was out of the town he quickly climbed onto the horse and galloped toward the foot of the hill where he had temporarily hidden his father's body.

Mai Mai was there waiting. She had brought incense and paper money, successfully "borrowed" from Mr. Ling. "I must go get a spade and a pick," Longevity said.

"I have brought them," Mai Mai said. "Let's start now, or the foreigners might catch us."

They put Ta Ming's body on the horse and struggled uphill immediately. The horse was strong and fast. Longevity had a hard time keeping up with it. He held the reins tightly to keep it from running away while Mai Mai held Ta Ming's body to keep it from slipping off.

There was still no sign of dawn when they reached the top of the hill. The area became more wooded, with pines growing thick and tall. The brush was dense. Longevity lost a shoe but it did not bother him. He was used to walking barefooted in China. He tossed the other shoe away and struggled on. The earth felt cool and rough under his feet. Thorny thickets poked at his ankles and knees. He liked it.

"This is far enough, Longevity," Mai Mai said. "You can hide anything here and nobody will ever find it."

Longevity stopped and looked around. It was indeed a fine spot for a temporary grave. There were tall pine trees and flowering bushes growing around rocks, just like those in China. He selected a secluded spot below some rocks, tied the horse to a bush and started digging. Mai Mai helped him with the spade.

They dug a shallow grave and buried the body, then leveled the top and covered it with dead leaves. In order to identify the grave, they collected small rocks and piled them under the closest pine.

Then they lighted the three sticks of incense and stuck them at the foot of the grave. Longevity knelt down in front of it and prayed. He promised his father's spirit solemnly that he would take his body back to China and bury it beside his ancestors, with due ceremony.

"Longevity," Mai Mai said excitedly, "take a close look at this! Quickly!"

Longevity looked into Mai Mai's outstretched hand. "What is it?" he asked.

"Look closer."

Longevity looked again. The egg-sized rock glowed slightly in the moonlight. "Gold nugget?" he asked.

"Rocks don't glow like this, Longevity."

"Where did you find it?"

"Right here, in the dirt we dug out of your father's grave."

Longevity picked up a handful of dirt. There was something hard in it. He worked his fingers until the dirt slipped away. What remained in his hands were chunks smaller than eggs, but they all glowed. He bent down and ran his fingers through the dirt. He picked up another rocklike piece and examined it closely. It glowed like the others.

"Look at this one," Mai Mai said. "As large as my

fist. We have made a strike, Longevity! We are rich!"

Tears came to Longevity's eyes. He sank down on his knees and kowtowed to the grave. "Father," he said, his voice choking, "you have answered my prayer."

"Let's burn the paper money," Mai Mai said. She brought out a stack of yellow paper from her pocket—coarse paper with small circles cut in it to represent coins.

Longevity lighted the paper money and kowtowed another time. Mai Mai also gave the grave a deep kowtow, touching the ground with her head.

The yellow paper burned quickly, lighting up the immediate area. Hundreds of gold nuggets glowed. Both Longevity and Mai Mai picked them up and pocketed them as fast as they could.

Soon the dead leaves began to burn. Frightened, they tried to stamp the fire out with their feet. Mai Mai's blouse caught fire. She threw herself on the ground and rolled until it was extinguished. "Get away from the fire," she shouted to Longevity, who was now beating the flames frantically with a stick. "Get away from it!"

Longevity didn't hear her. Now the fire began to spread. Mai Mai grabbed Longevity and pulled him away. "Do you want to be burned alive?" she cried.

"Where is the horse?"

"The horse has better sense than you and me," Mai Mai said, dragging Longevity away from the fire. "It knows when to run for its life. Let's go, you fool!"

Tumbling and fighting bushes, they ran down the slope. By the time they reached the other side of the hill the fire was leaping toward the sky, burning trees and brush. Mai Mai, her clothes torn, sat down under an oak tree and hugged herself, breathless. Longevity sank beside her, exhausted, his hands and feet bleeding. "Well, we've made a strike," he said breathlessly.

"Longevity," Mai Mai said, "can you lend me your blouse?"

"Are you cold?"

"Mine is torn to pieces. I can't hide myself."

Longevity took off his blouse. "What shall we do with our gold?"

"We won't hit wild dogs with it," Mai Mai said, taking Longevity's blouse. "Please turn away."

"Why?"

"There is something you don't know about me. Turn away, please."

Longevity turned away and Mai Mai put on his blouse. The sky began to glow behind the eastern mountains. "It is dawn," Longevity said. "I can't go back now."

"Why not?" Mai Mai said. "We can pretend we have been looking for your father's body."

"No, we can't. I have lost one of Mr. Carnahan's horses and burned a mountain. The foreigners are sure to hang me. You go back, Straw Sandal. You can pretend that you have been looking for me."

"What are you going to do?" Mai Mai asked.

"I don't know. But I cannot go back to the camp."

"Don't forget, you are in a foreign country."

"I have learned the foreign tongue and I have some gold. I shall manage."

"Maybe you are right," Mai Mai said. "And we

have made a strike. Only you and I know where it is. Why should we go back?"

"We can go to another town," Longevity said. "We can stay there until the foreigners have forgotten about us. Then we can come back here to get my father's body and the gold."

Mai Mai thought for a moment and said with a sigh, "Maybe it is the will of your father. How much do you know about the foreign talk?"

"I understand more than half of it. And I can swear a lot."

"Your father wouldn't like to hear you swear."

"Mr. Carnahan swears. He is respected by everybody."

"Well, perhaps you know better," Mai Mai said. "I have a confession to make, Longevity. You can look at me now."

Longevity turned. Mai Mai had put on his blouse and tossed her own away. "I am a woman, Longevity."

Longevity stared at her for a moment. "You are still Straw Sandal."

"I am not. I disguised myself as a boy when I joined the group. I am a woman. Seventeen years old. Are you disappointed?"

Longevity did not know what to say. He had always thought Straw Sandal behaved a little strangely. Now he knew why. "Do you still want me to go with you, Longevity?"

"I don't mind. Is that why you never wash your face?"

"Certainly I wash my face," Mai Mai said, offended. "I wash my face every day. But I smear a little dirt on it to look more like a boy. And I pretend to snore, too."

"What shall I call you now?" Longevity asked.

"Call me Straw Sandal. I shall tell you my real name when the day comes that I can wear a woman's clothes again. I am not an ugly girl, Longevity. When I dress up like a woman you will not be ashamed to call me sister. That is what we shall do. When we go back to China rich, you will call me older sister and I shall call you younger brother."

"You have a younger brother."

"No, I don't. My younger brother died. I have nobody. Since then, I have wanted another younger brother. That's why I lied."

Longevity moved closer to her. "I'll be your younger brother," he said with a shy smile.

Mai Mai took his hand. "You are the man in the family now, Longevity. From now on you will do the talking and make the decisions."

The sun had just risen, shining warmly on both of them. In the hills the fire was burning fiercely.

22

For two days Longevity and Mai Mai fled along a lonely trail without any idea of where they were going. They travelled by night, slept in bushes by day, and staved off starvation by eating wild berries and bird eggs. At the end of the second day they caught a rabbit, discussed how to cook it and decided to do it beggar-style. Longevity remembered that Four-eyed Dog had told him how a beggar cooks a duck. They built a small fire, packed the rabbit in mud and threw the mudball into the fire. They kept the fire going until the mudball became hardened. Then they cracked the mudball open and ate the rabbit ravenously. After sundown they started the journey again, hoping to find a town and a bed. Longevity's fear of being caught was now diluted by his hunger for a Chinese meal.

When they came to a wider trail, they turned into it. The road took them into a small village of tents and log cabins. Having made sure they had not returned to Hangtown in a roundabout way, they decided to go through the town to try to find a Chinese restaurant. Longevity had heard from Mr. Quon that there were Chinese in this foreign land who had come before the gold rush and had been selling a food called "chop suey." He had never heard of chop suey in China but he was sure those Chinese would also sell real Chinese food. Mai Mai agreed, swallowing at the thought of a Chinese dinner.

It was early morning and the town was still quiet. They saw a few miners walking on the street—probably going to work. Longevity stopped the first man they met and asked him his carefully prepared question. The man looked at him curiously for a moment, then smiled, pointed to the west and said something that Longevity did not quite understand.

But the pointing was good enough. Longevity and Mai Mai followed the road going west. They did not find any Chinese restaurants, but the road took them to San Francisco.

They stood on top of a hill and looked down at the bay. It was late afternoon and the sinking sun had set the distant water aflame. There were rocks in the bay covered with seals and sea lions. On the right they saw blue mountains rising behind bluer mountains. Fog drifted through them, like a Chinese painting. When they came down the hill, the road widened and the traffic became busier. They proceeded cautiously, hiding in the bushes every time large groups of people came by—especially men riding on horses.

Suddenly they saw a wagon approaching, pulled by a middle-aged Chinese. He looked like a friendly man with a smiling moon face. He pulled the cart with a leather belt strapped to his shoulders. The small cart was loaded with vegetables, a duck, two chickens, and a Pekingese dog. Longevity came out of hiding and greeted him pleasantly in Cantonese.

The man's face brightened as if he were happy to see another Chinese. *"Wei, wei,* what wind has blown a fellow countryman here?" he asked jovially.

Longevity introduced himself politely. Mai Mai came out of the brush and waited at a distance. "Ah," the Chinese said, "Lucky day. Two fellow countrymen. Call me Number Nine. The foreigners call me John Chinaman. Every Chinese is John in this foreign land. They cannot tell one John from another."

"We have been looking for a Chinese restaurant," Longevity said. "A foreigner pointed to the west. We have travelled two days in this direction and still have not come across it yet."

"He directed you correctly," Number Nine said. "Only in San Francisco can you find a Chinese restaurant. Follow me, please."

Longevity and Mai Mai followed him. Number Nine proved to be a jolly man who loved to talk. "My donkey is sick today," he said. "So I am substituting for him. He caught cold—the donkey—passed on by the Pekingese. Watch the dog sneeze. I sell everything on the cart except the Pekingese. But sometimes the Pekingese is the only thing the foreigners want to buy. And I have a good mind to sell it."

The dog sneezed. Mai Mai laughed. It was the first time Longevity had heard Mai Mai laugh. Suddenly he could not help laughing too. He had not laughed for so long that the laughter made him feel good. It made him forget the lingering sadness of his father's death.

"The dog has been chasing the donkey," Number Nine said. "But the donkey has another donkey in mind. That is why I have brought the dog. The donkey deserves some peace and quiet without being annoyed by a female dog.

"She is a jealous one, this dog, and has a temper. I call her Lotus Blossom. I gave her a pretty name to please her. She likes it. Watch her prick up her ears when I call her."

Number Nine called Lotus Blossom twice and the dog sneezed.

"She has a cold," Number Nine went on. "She can't hear too well when she has a cold. Where are you from, fellow countrymen?"

"I am from a village near Canton," Longevity said. "Straw Sandal is from a village in Toy Shan District."

"I am from Toy Shan District, too," Number Nine said excitedly. "There are five fellow countrymen in San Francisco, all from Toy Shan. They are acrobats-turned-cooks. Every Chinese is a John and a cook now. No good. So I sell vegetables. I was a magician. I could produce a frog from my sleeve and swallow it. But the foreigners wanted me to swallow fire and knives and snakes. I quit."

Presently they reached the ferry landing. Number Nine pulled his cart onto the ferryboat and paid the fare for himself and his guests with silver coins. The vast bay was full of boats of all sizes. The seals and sea lions sunning themselves on the rocks ignored the noisy seagulls flapping and pecking around them.

When the ferryboat approached San Francisco, Mai Mai could see the city clearly. There were thousands of canvas tents and houses on the flat that extended for some distance along the shores of the cove. Behind them rose the hills.

They went ashore at a landing built on a beach of deep black sand. The beach was covered with wreckage —levers, cranks, cogwheels, twisted bars and all types of rusted iron. "All labor-saving gold-washing machines," Number Nine said. "They could no more wash gold than my donkey could play a game of mahjong. That's the only thing you can steal here without getting strung up—these machines. Have you been to the gold country?"

"No," Longevity said quickly.

"Everybody goes to the mines. I would, too, if it weren't for a bandit who likes to string up Chinese by their queues. That is Three-fingered Jack's only hobby and entertainment."

"Have you seen him?" Longevity asked.

"Merciful Buddha, no!"

"I heard about the crimson-colored men who like to eat the front part of a human head," Longevity said. "Is that true?"

"They may not eat it, but they sure like to preserve it. But have no fear fellow countrymen, the Indians are not as vicious as they say. Only the other day a white man told me, 'Number Nine, I don't know how God created you Chinamen, but I know this: a red man will scalp his enemy; a white man will skin his friend.' That's what he said. He was a miner. Somebody stole his horse; another man jumped his claim; a friend fleeced him of all his money. Now he is a dishwasher in a Chinese restaurant. By the way, have you come for the gold rush?"

"No," Longevity said hastily.

"You don't have to deny it so heatedly," Number Nine said, casting him a suspicious glance. "There is lots of room in the gold country. Anybody can stake a claim just by throwing his pick and spade on the ground. But I wouldn't go for all the gold in the world. Three-fingered Jack is good enough reason for me to sell vegetables."

Presently they reached the main street. It was the first time since her arrival in the foreign country that Mai Mai had seen so many permanent buildings and so many people. It was almost like the streets in China. There were little men, big men, fat men, dirty men, clean men—most of them dressed in red shirts and pantaloons tucked into the tops of their boots. Some of them wore broad belts with silver buckles and floppy old hats. A few looked more dignified, sporting shiny top hats.

There were mountains of goods lying in open sheds and buildings still under construction—calico, silk, furniture, iron stoves, sacks of flour, and many other items covered with dust and mud. According to Number Nine, it was the cargoes dumped by ships now idling in the bay. The local merchants could buy them cheaply but found no place to store them.

"Anybody who has a shack on this street," Number Nine said, "is mining gold right here. He can rent it for a thousand dollars a month. Watch out, don't step into that large box of tobacco. The owner might jump out from around the corner, grab you and make you pay for it. That's the best way to get rid of unwanted merchandise these days."

The street led them to the plaza called Portsmouth Square. It was a busy lot of land surrounded by permanent buildings. There were saloons, hotels, restaurants and government houses. Among the people coming and going, Mai Mai spotted a rich Chinese dressed in a loose brocade gown with large sleeves. He walked slowly, his hands tucked in his loose sleeves, his face serene. People looked at him curiously, but the Chinese sauntered along, without looking to his right or left. Number Nine greeted him pleasantly. The Chinese grunted his greeting in return.

"He is a cook," Number Nine said. "Now he has so much money he has become high class, dresses himself like a Mandarin and grunts a lot. That is his stage costume, mind you. He was one of the acrobats, too old to tumble or stand on his head. He became rich because of Three-fingered Jack."

"Why?" Longevity asked.

"If not for the bandit, his own hired cooks would have gone to the gold country to wash clothes for the miners. They could make a lot more money than cooking for a restaurant. Oh, that reminds me, you are looking for a Chinese restaurant. I was going to take you to the largest, owned by this turtle whom I just greeted. But I didn't like the way he grunted, so I'll take you to the best, instead."

They turned a corner. On a side street they saw a Chinese sign saying, "The Restaurant of Ten Thousand Flowers." "The English sign says 'chop suey,'" Number Nine said. "That's something to fool the foreigners. When the cooks make chop suey they hold their noses. But the foreigners like it. They have strange tastes."

"Have you tried it?" Longevity asked.

"Me? Nobody can make me walk within ten feet of a bowl of chop suey. Not even Three-fingered Jack."

"Does it smell?"

"Worse than that. It is tasteless—the greatest catastrophe in food. In the art of cuisine, it is in the same category as being poisonous. But the foreigners like it. That turtle's egg whom I just greeted has made a fortune out of it. Here it is, the best Chinese restaurant in San Francisco, where the owner is still his own cook. He was an acrobat too. Broke his leg. He might be a little slow, but he cooks well."

They arrived at the small restaurant. Number Nine parked his cart beside the door. The restaurant was gaudily decorated with Chinese lanterns, an embroidery of peacocks and rocks, and a few pots of flowers with lucky sayings pasted on them. There were about ten tables in the narrow room, mostly occupied by miners in red shirts.

Number Nine took Longevity and Mai Mai to an empty table in a corner near the door. A young waiter came to the table with a pot of tea and three cups. He greeted Number Nine like an old friend. "How is business?" the waiter asked.

"Made one sale this morning, to an old customer who did not have any money," Number Nine said cheerfully. "But he paid me with two chickens and a duck. Go ask your father if he wants them. And ask him to prepare three or four dishes for two fellow countrymen."

"It takes time."

"Who is in a hurry?"

After the waiter had left, Number Nine poured tea. Suddenly Longevity leaped up and bolted out of the door. "What's wrong with him?" Number Nine asked with a frown.

"I'll find out," Mai Mai said. She ran out and found Longevity scurrying down the street, his head turning and his pigtail flying. Mai Mai caught up with him and grabbed him by the sleeve.

"Run, older sister," Longevity said breathlessly. "I saw a man who looked like Mr. Carnahan."

"Where?"

"In that restaurant."

"Are you sure?"

"I'm not near-sighted."

"I did not see him," Mai Mai said.

"He was sitting in the other corner," Longevity said. "Lucky he did not see us."

Number Nine had come out and was now chasing

them. *"Wei, wei,* fellow countrymen," he yelled, "wait! If you think I am going to treat you to chop suey, you're wrong!"

When he caught them, Longevity explained why he had run.

"That's what I thought," Number Nine said. "You two came from the gold country. You have that look in your faces. All miners have it—haunted by greed and fear. Well, don't be afraid, fellow countrymen. If that Mr. Carnahan is eating chop suey in that restaurant, he must have left his mine for the usual reason—being flat broke. It should not cause you and your friend any concern. Except perhaps you may have to pay for his dinner. But today you are my guests."

"We borrowed his horse and lost it," Longevity said.

Number Nine's face fell. "That's different," he said seriously. "You'd better hide at my place for a few days. I'll go get my cart." He dashed back to the restaurant, his pigtail flapping.

"Does he wear boots?" Mai Mai asked.

"Yes, black boots covered with mud."

"Mr. Carnahan never wears dirty boots. Let's go back."

Just as Mai Mai was trying to drag Longevity back, Number Nine came running with his cart, which bumped on the rough road, clippety-clapping. Lotus Blossom was barking.

"We are not afraid, Number Nine," Mai Mai said. "We are going back."

"Run, fellow countrymen, run!" Number Nine

yelled. "A white man likes nothing better than to string up a man who borrows his horse!"

At that moment a fat Chinese came limping, waving a meat cleaver. *"Wei,* Number Nine," he shouted. "What's the matter? Why do you run like that? Is there a plague in my restaurant?"

"I'll pay for the dinner, Lee Sin," Number Nine said, quickly digging his hand into his pocket.

"What dinner?" Lee Sin asked. "You did not eat my dinner and I did not cook it. What about your two chickens and the duck? Why did you escape? Do you think I could not pay?" He dug out a little pouch from his pocket and poured some gold dust onto Number Nine's hand. "Here it is—about an ounce. If it is not enough, I'll call you a name that you won't like."

With that, he grabbed the chicken coop and limped back to his restaurant, the alarmed chickens cackling and the duck quacking.

"Well, lucky day," Number Nine said, looking at the gold dust. "They say Lee Sin always pays more if you run. That's no exaggeration."

23

Longevity and Mai Mai found Number Nine to be friendly and hospitable. His two-room shack on the hill was built of redwood, tidily furnished with home-made chairs, a table and some crates.

"Three crates make a bed," Number Nine said. "When the wife comes from China, I can just add three more crates in the bedroom and a pair of chopsticks on the table. She will be the first Chinese woman to set her feet in this new land."

Number Nine enjoyed talking and was happy to find

two listeners. He had come to America with an acrobatic troupe sponsored by an American businessman who had recently died.

"When I stopped being a magician, I became Mr. Parker's Number Nine boy," he said. "He had eight other cooks who all died of drinking and overeating. Mr. Parker survived them all. He lived to ninety-three. Died in his sleep with a smile on his face. He could have survived me if I had taken to drinking. Mr. Parker had all kinds of rare liquors and delicacies, and he let his servants keep the key. That was a mistake. The eight servants before me all died of greed. Eight dead cooks is lesson enough for the number nine. That's why I'm a teetotaler." He lowered his voice and added with a mischievous smile, "But I make it up with other vices. You are too young to know what they are."

He cooked a good dinner—fried salted fish, mushrooms with chicken feet, taro roots brewed with garlic leaf, and octopus fingers fried with Chinese cabbage. Longevity ate three bowls of rice and belched in appreciation. Mai Mai, in order to behave like a man, did likewise.

"I have made some homemade wine for guests, but I won't serve you," Number Nine said. "If you did not have a white man chasing you, I would say go ahead and have a jar. But when you are in trouble, it is better to keep your head clear and know where you are going in case you must run. Well, I hope you will be safe here. People seldom come to this hill except when they're looking for mushrooms. Good poisonous mushrooms are hard to get. But they are the best way to kill a friend and jump his claim. If you see a man hunting for mushrooms on this hill, you can be sure he is a miner planning to murder a friend."

"You don't think we are crooks, do you, Number Nine?" Longevity asked.

"You don't look like one. Nor does your friend," Number Nine said. "But even if you had stolen somebody's horse, I would still help you. Fellow countrymen must all stick together in a foreign land. Besides, the horse ran away. A professional horse thief would never let that happen.

"But don't ever let anybody know you have touched somebody else's horse. In this foreign land it is worse than touching somebody's wife. People in this country have strange rules. They think our customs are peculiar. They laugh at our queues. The other day a man asked me, 'Hey, Number Nine, how big are your wife's bound feet?' I told him the truth—three and a half inches. The man doubled up laughing. I asked him how big his wife's feet are. He said about the size of a ten-pound catfish. Have you ever seen a foreign woman's feet? Ten pounds apiece, at least. No exaggeration. And they look like catfish, too. Well, have another bowl of rice and finish the dishes. I must go back to town and sell more vegetables."

"You must let us pay for your hospitality," Longevity said.

"Don't think of it," Number Nine said, rising from the crude wooden table. "You have already made some money for me—an ounce of gold to be exact—by running. I only expected Lee Sin to pay me half an ounce of gold for the chickens and the duck—or eight dollars, to be exact."

At the door Number Nine added, "However, I'll let you feed my donkey and keep an eye on Lotus Blossom. The dog eats rice. Keep her in the house so she can't annoy the donkey. I suspect that the donkey is worried sick. Nothing is worse than having a Pekingese chasing a donkey amorously. You can see the result; the master winds up pulling the donkey cart."

With a bow, Number Nine left his guests.

Longevity and Mai Mai stayed at Number Nine's shack for a week without stepping outside. Every day Number Nine would bring back Chinese mustard greens, bean sprouts, bitter melon, and other Chinese vegetables. Longevity had never enjoyed eating so much.

Number Nine also brought home the news of the day, such as that stagecoach service had just started between the gold country and San Francisco; a hanging had taken place in the morning; a new medicine man had arrived at Portsmouth Square selling a miracle medicine that could help any man grow a decent mustache, and so forth.

In fact, Number Nine talked about Portsmouth Square so often that Longevity's desire to visit the place became stronger every day. He wanted to visit the saloon, eat a foreign meal, or just stand around watching people. He decided to do all these things by himself. In case he saw Mr. Carnahan or Mr. King, he could run or hide more easily without having to drag a girl with him. If he got caught, it would be his fate. Besides, since Straw Sandal had become a girl, he often found himself a little shy when talking to her. Their relationship was not the same anymore.

He told Mai Mai what was on his mind.

"Longevity," Mai Mai said, "if you must visit this Portsmouth Square by yourself, will you buy four yards of calico, some thread and needles for me?"

"What do you want all these things for?"

"To keep myself busy."

"But don't let Number Nine see you sewing. You know how he talks."

"I'll only do it when I'm alone, and when he comes back I'll hide everything. I won't even let you see me sewing."

Longevity turned to the window and stared out. "Are you homesick, Straw Sandal?"

"A little, why?"

"My father has probably become impatient in that shallow grave by now," he said. "No incense, no offerings from relatives. When he looks around, there is nothing but charred trees and burned grass."

"But he is buried in gold, Longevity."

"Spirits may not care for real gold. I wish I could take him back to China right now. I want to have his body properly buried in our ancestral burial grounds before his spirit becomes too unhappy."

"We'll find a partner and go mine our gold, Longevity. What do you think of Number Nine?"

"We don't know him well."

"He looks like an honest man."

"We'll wait two months. Wait till we know him better."

"I'm a woman, Longevity. You are a man. You make the decision."

Longevity hitched up his trousers like a man. "We'll go mine our gold, don't worry."

Mai Mai had tried not to think of Mr. Carnahan, but the sudden thought that she might not see him again saddened her.

"You look sad, older sister. Why?"

"I'm homesick too, Longevity."

"Don't forget, we are very rich."

"Oh, that reminds me," Mai Mai said. "Don't buy calico. Please buy four yards of silk. I like sky blue."

When Longevity went to buy the silk, he could not help smiling. Mai Mai had twice called him a man. That made him very happy. He suddenly felt two feet taller. Taking a deep breath he strode toward Portsmouth Square with his chest high and head up. He decided to buy a gun first—the kind Mr. Carnahan carried, with a fancy ivory handle.

When he passed a gunshop he saw miners in it—bearded men dressed like Mr. Carnahan and Mr. King. Not willing to take a chance, he hurried on.

Portsmouth Square was as busy as ever. Medicine men in black suits and top hats talked and gesticulated behind stalls. Men in old shirts and dusty boots hurried in and out of shops, restaurants and saloons, or walked aimlessly, or just stood around loafing and chewing tobacco. A few Indians squatted in a corner smoking and staring at nothing. Mule carts driven by Mexicans came and went. A well-dressed man in silk coat and vest rode through leisurely, tipping his hat to a tall woman walking her poodle.

Longevity enjoyed the sights and the mixed smells of

horse manure and perfume. He spent a gold nugget like a man—a nugget that weighed almost an ounce. He bought a felt hat for himself, four yards of the best silk for Mai Mai. It was hard to get needles and thread, but the cloth merchant who sold him the silk borrowed his wife's sewing box, fished out the items and stuffed them into Longevity's pocket when his wife wasn't looking. He said he had never talked to a Chinaman before, and that it was an honor to present the last two items as a gift to his first Chinese customer.

Longevity thoroughly enjoyed the morning. Before returning to the hill he went past the gunsmith. The shop was still crowded. He decided to come early next time. Buying a gun was not like buying a hat or silk; it was important business; he mustn't do it casually.

Mai Mai was delighted with the sewing material. It would keep her mind off Hangtown and Mr. Carnahan. Immediately she shut herself in the other room and plunged into her feminine work. She did not emerge from the room until she heard Number Nine's voice.

"Good news," Number Nine said excitedly as he shuffled into the shack. "I sold my donkey and my cart. A white man paid me ten ounces of gold for them. He was either crazy or drunk."

"How are you going to sell vegetables now, Number Nine?" Longevity asked.

"I'm going into the laundry business with a friend. This friend has been fooling the foreigners with chop suey for so long that his conscience began to bother him. He hopes that washing their clothes will atone for his sin. Besides, he can make more money. We can get a lot of business from the gold country. Some miners in the gold country even send their laundry to Hawaii to be washed. Everybody washes gold these days and nobody washes clothes. So my friend and I are going into the laundry business."

"We are going to miss the donkey," Mai Mai said.

"The donkey will be happier," Number Nine said. "At least he will have no female dog chasing him. Oh, I'd like you to meet a foreign lady tomorrow. She is a missionary woman. Lived in China for twenty years. She is the only foreigner who does not call every Chinese 'John.' She teaches English."

"I know the foreign talk," Longevity said.

"Who taught you?"

"The sailors on a foreign ship."

"If you learned the foreign talk from sailors or miners," Number Nine said, "you need Miss Randall to clean it up for you. She teaches English free of charge."

Number Nine had a great deal to say about Miss Randall. He said that she had a temper, but only lost it on her own people. One day a white man was cussing a Chinese cook in a Chinese restaurant and smashing rice bowls. Miss Randall came in, picked up a bowl of chop suey and poured it on the troublemaker's head. Then she grabbed his beard, dragged him outside and gave him a kick in the shin before she told him off. The man limped away meekly. When Miss Randall came back to the restaurant, everybody applauded her, including the one whose chop suey she had borrowed. "A real good friend of the Chinese, Miss Randall," Number Nine concluded. "She shoots and rides horseback, too. And her kick is bigger than a mule's."

Next morning Number Nine took Longevity and Mai Mai to see Miss Randall. She was a stout, middle-aged lady with gray hair, who wore a large man's watch on a brass chain around her neck. Her eyes were bright and sharp, and she had a habit of looking at people with her head lowered as though she was peering over a pair of invisible glasses.

In her large two-room cabin she taught English and conducted weekly religious services. The main room was crowded with chairs, books, blackboards, an organ, and a table. In the back was a small statue of Christ facing the entrance. Number Nine introduced his new friends with a big grin. Miss Randall received the visitors with several nods. "Do you wish to learn the foreign talk?" she asked in Chinese, peering at Longevity and Mai Mai over her invisible glasses.

"They have learned the foreign talk from sailors," Number Nine said. "They want you to clean it up for them."

"The fastest way to clean up a man's language is to fine him half a dollar every time he swears," Miss Randall said. "Do you have money?"

"Yes, Madam," Longevity said.

"Good. The money will go into the till for my missionary service in China. Advanced English classes three evenings a week. In the class nobody speaks Chinese. Every time you speak a word of Chinese, a fine of half a dollar is charged. If you have no money, a cross will be marked under your name in my roll book. If anybody has collected ten crosses, he has two choices—either clean this cabin or wash my dishes for three weeks. Do you write?"

"No, Madam," Longevity said.

Miss Randall wrote their names down in her roll book. "All right, classes start next Wednesday evening at eight. Don't be late. Now business is over; it is time to be sociable. Jasmine tea or black dragon tea?"

They had black dragon tea which Miss Randall made in a large coffeepot. She also served homemade biscuits and roasted watermelon seeds. During the tea, Miss Randall preached the gospels of Christ and talked about the evils of gambling. She hated gambling of any kind. She said that if she had any authority or power, she would invade the saloons, especially the Bella Union at Portsmouth Square. She would smash every gambling table with an ax, haul all the gamblers to the street and give every one of them a kick in the shin with her iron-tipped shoes. When she talked she gave Number Nine a significant glance that made Number Nine lower his eyes and look cowed.

Miss Randall also talked about her great ambition— to build the first Chinatown in America. She had heard that many Chinese had come to California for the gold rush. Her prediction was that when the rush was over, many would remain. If so, it would be her job to see that they learned the proper English and settled down in San Francisco as useful citizens, and her iron-tipped shoes would see to it that nobody cheated them of their hard-earned gold.

When everybody finished his tea, Miss Randall looked at her enormous watch, rose quickly and said, "All right, it is time for you to go. If you have any problems with my people, come to me. Stand up for your rights. Only run when your dear life is threatened.

If someone slaps you on one cheek, don't turn the other, as most missionaries preach. What do you do? Kick him in the shin. Christ would approve, in my opinion. Remember this place well. Don't walk into somebody else's cabin when you come next time. One Chinese did last week and he was almost lynched. One always suspects others of being a thief these days. Everybody has a little gold hidden somewhere—that is why. Goodbye."

She stepped outside and accepted the visitors' polite bows with three nods and a flicker of a smile.

24

Mai Mai liked the English class. There were five students and she was the only one who had not been fined so far. Longevity was fined only once for swearing. He was proud of the record, although he missed the rough talk. Swearing was like juggling a gun—it delighted him and made him feel that he was like Mr. Carnahan.

Number Nine's business partner, Iron Head Mah, was the slowest learner. He used to sit in the class quietly, like a hunk of clay. When Miss Randall found out that he did not speak a word of English, she promptly switched him to the beginners' class. Iron Head did his best. He spoke the simplest words as though he had a hot potato in his mouth; and when he finished a word he looked as though he had just swallowed the potato, his face red and eyes crossed. Number Nine said Iron Head had once been a good acrobat and was now an excellent laundryman. Too bad he just couldn't learn the foreign talk.

Number Nine decided to give his business partner extra lessons in English after work, so that he could at least greet customers properly. After a few weeks of hard work Iron Head had learned several greetings, but nobody could be sure what he really meant until after two or three guesses. The only greeting that Iron Head spoke without too much effort was "How are you?" which he handily pronounced as "aiyoo," which meant "ouch" in Chinese. When Number Nine talked about it, he always shook his head sadly.

At Miss Randall's cabin Iron Head studied even harder, always mumbling new words to himself. Miss Randall declared that she was an impatient woman, but she was also stubborn; she would make Iron Head learn the foreign talk no matter what, even though she had already developed muscles from throwing up her arms in despair.

Number Nine had already graduated, but he went occasionally to the advanced class for a brush-up lesson. He spoke English with a heavy accent and sometimes with Chinese grammar, but Miss Randall considered it no great blasphemy to the English language and made no effort to correct his mistakes, except a few words such as "rice." She didn't want Number Nine to go around saying, "Yes, I eat lice." There was already a rumor spreading in San Francisco that the Chinese ate lice. Miss Randall was sure Number Nine was responsible for it.

However, Number Nine's laundry business was booming. His hands had become reddish and roughened, but the gold dust, the silver and gold coins that rolled into the till more than compensated for the hardships. Sometimes he missed his donkey.

"Wonder where the beast is now," he would say. "He likes tumbleweed, the fool. He is of low breed but friendly. He never kicked me. When he lost his temper he only snorted, humph, humph, humph. A dignified donkey, except when he was depressed. Who would not be depressed if he were chased by Lotus Blossom, a bitch not larger than a donkey's ear?"

When Number Nine missed the donkey, he always expressed his sentiment in the same manner, with hardly a change of words. After two weeks Mai Mai could repeat it word for word. She was annoyed, but she listened to him politely, trying to let the words go into one ear and come out the other. Sometimes it was not easy.

She became more talkative. It made her feel better. She was glad that her high-pitched voice had not made Number Nine suspicious of her sex. It was probably because Number Nine hardly listened when others were talking.

It took her three weeks to finish her sewing. One morning, after Number Nine had gone to work, she decided to do something she had a burning desire to do—

be a woman again. When she came out of the other room dressed like a woman, Longevity turned sharply. She wore her new shiny gown of sky blue with loose sleeves. Her long silk trousers showed under her gown, covering her feet. Her hair was oiled and braided in a bun that was piled on top of her head. Her face was clean, her eyes sparkling. Holding Lotus Blossom in one hand, she walked mincingly to the center of the room, turned and smiled with a finger touching her cheek coquettishly. "How do you like my dress, Longevity? I made it with the material you bought for me."

Longevity stared at her, dumbfounded.

"Say something, Longevity. Don't watch me with your mouth wide open like an empty vegetable bowl. Today I am a woman, your real older sister. My name is Mai Mai. I want you to take me out this morning. We shall take a walk in town."

"I . . . I don't know you," Longevity stammered.

"Of course you don't know me. I am a woman now."

"What if Number Nine sees you like this?"

"What of it? I'll give him a piece of my mind. Oh, how I enjoy being a woman again! Now I want strangers to look at me. I want men to whisper comments about me to one another. I want them to turn their heads after I have passed. When Number Nine comes back, I want to say to him, 'You silly man, how do you know it was not that ugly donkey who has been chasing Lotus Blossom? So please shut up from now on and have more respect for a female!' "

"You even talk differently," Longevity said, still staring at her.

"Longevity, no woman chases a man; a woman only

leads him on. Every time Number Nine talks about Lotus Blossom chasing that old donkey, I want to hit him on the head with my rice bowl. Now let's go out and see the world."

Longevity consented reluctantly, feeling somewhat self-conscious as they went down the hill. Mai Mai walked with her head high, busily glancing to her right and left. She was enjoying the attention and blushing with excitement. For the first time in almost a year she felt like a woman again.

Longevity was uneasy. But when he passed a new gunshop, his attention was immediately attracted by the rich display of revolvers, shotguns and rifles of different sizes and designs. He tugged at Mai Mai's sleeve. They stopped and looked into the shop for a moment. Longevity stared at the guns and kept taking long breaths until he worked up enough courage to walk into the shop. He bought a gun with a white ivory handle. It cost him two gold nuggets, but it was the closest thing he could find to Mr. Carnahan's gun.

He also bought a holster and a wide belt with a silver buckle. He wore the gun belt under his blouse with the gun hanging down on his side. Stepping out onto the street, he looked to his right and left, greatly thrilled. The gun slapped his thigh annoyingly as he walked, but the weight felt good. Even though it had a tendency to slip down over his hips, it did not matter. He could easily reach for the gun without cocking his arm. Only occasionally the gun would drag his trousers down, but he solved that problem by walking with an upward jerk. When the gun and the trousers reached the danger point of slipping all the way down, he would jerk them up and quickly expand his stomach to keep them from falling. Then he would walk with his stomach and chest expanded until the gun and the trousers began to slip again.

The upward jerk looked a little funny but Mai Mai did not mention it. She was too busy glancing around and enjoying herself.

They walked toward Portsmouth Square attracting a great deal of attention. Some people turned and smiled. Others halted in their tracks and stared. A few tipped their hats in salute and greeted them in a jovial tone. Three men tugged their beards and made remarks that Mai Mai did not understand. One put his big hands on his hips, looked at them and guffawed.

But nobody followed them until they reached Portsmouth Square. First two men, then four, then half a dozen followed them, talking and laughing. Longevity began to feel nervous. Mai Mai enjoyed it all the more; she walked with her chin pointing higher and her steps more mincing. She pulled a long face, her eyes shifting from one side to the other.

"We're being followed," Longevity whispered.

Mai Mai looked at him askance with a flicker of a smile. "Why don't you turn and say 'boo,' Longevity?" she whispered back merrily.

"You are so changed. I don't know you."

"That's good. I don't want to look like Straw Sandal now that I am Mai Mai. That's my real name, Longevity. I promised to tell you that, didn't I?"

"Could you walk without mincing like that?" Longevity whispered, a little embarrassed.

"Could you walk without jumping like a rabbit?"

"I'm not jumping. I'm only trying to keep my trousers up."

"I'm only walking the way I used to walk in my village."

"Too much swaying."

"Men like it," Mai Mai said. "You are not a man yet, Longevity. You'll like it in two or three years."

Longevity glanced back and became more worried. More than a dozen men were following them now. "We'd better go back," he said.

"For a whole year nobody so much as glanced at me," Mai Mai said. "Now I want a hundred men to follow me."

"Are you insane?"

"You are a coward, Longevity. I thought you were a brave boy."

Longevity resented the remark, but he did not want to start a quarrel in the middle of the street. He walked and jerked and felt more uneasy. Now he wondered if the men behind them were laughing at his jerking movement or at Mai Mai's mincing steps. He wished he had asked the gunsmith to punch an extra hole in his gun belt. He had expanded his stomach so much that it began to grumble and he found it hard to breathe freely under such circumstances.

Before they reached the Bella Union a noisy man with a large black beard caught up with them from behind, talking and laughing loudly. He was a big man with a square face and bushy eyebrows and a gold tooth gleaming in his untidy beard. He wore a dirty red shirt, a broad-brimmed hat, tight sheepskin trousers, dusty black boots and a gun. His hands were hairy and rough, bearing the marks of many healed wounds. He walked alongside Mai Mai. Every time he made a funny remark the men following shouted and laughed.

"Hey, ma'am," the man said, bowing low to Mai Mai with his hat off, "may I have the pleasure of escorting you to the Bella Union for a drink? Let me be the first man to bring a Chinese doll to an American saloon and introduce to the drinking public the most esteemed Chinese culture—your honorable small bound feet—if you have small bound feet, that is, ma'am."

He took out his gun and fired a shot into the sky. "I salute Chinese womanhood, and all the small bound feet in China."

The people trailing behind laughed. The man fired another shot as if to applaud himself. Then he holstered the gun, turned to his audience and took several bows.

"Ma'am," he went on, grinning broadly when he caught up with Mai Mai again, "it is my life's great desire to see a pair of Chinese bound feet. I'm ready to make bets with anyone who is willing to risk ten ounces of gold and say that a Chinese woman's bound foot is no smaller than six inches. I say it is no larger than five inches. Ten ounces of pure gold, anyone?"

There was more laughter, but no takers for the bet. The man repeated his challenge a few times and fired another shot into the air. Longevity became more nervous. Alternately he grinned and bit his lower lip. Mai Mai walked with her head higher, enjoying every moment. Longevity glanced at her. She pulled a long face, but there was a glitter of merriment in her eyes. Longevity didn't like it.

"All right, you cowards," the man shouted at the trailing crowd. "I'll switch the bets with you. I'll say this China doll's small bound feet are larger than five inches. Ten ounces of gold, anyone?"

"I'll bet you a bottle of whiskey on that," a miner shouted from the group.

"Bottle of whiskey it is," the bearded man shouted back. "A bottle of whiskey to be shared by this Chinese beauty at the Bella Union. Anyone who wants to join the party buys his own drinks. Now, ma'am, may we have the pleasure of taking a look at your honorable small bound feet?"

"They say you have big feet," Longevity whispered to Mai Mai.

"Certainly I have big feet. I was a farmer's daughter," Mai Mai whispered back.

"They want to look."

"I won't let them! That's why I cover them with my trouser legs. No one is going to look at my feet!"

"Hey, China doll, ma'am," the bearded man said, "will you show us your honorable small bound feet, please? I've bet a whole bottle of good whiskey with a gentleman on the size. Now be a good sport and show them. Please, ma'am, show your lotus petals. Win or lose you are my guest. We'll all have a bottle of whiskey at the Bella Union. Hey, China doll, show your blasted petals! Don't keep the gentleman waiting!"

As the man bent down to lift Mai Mai's trousers,

Mai Mai dug her fingernails viciously into his face. He leaped back with a groan, stunned. Then he touched his bleeding face with a hand and snarled.

Now a big crowd was following them. Some were laughing and some shouting "Bravo!" With a curse the man drew his gun. Longevity whipped out his and fired, knocking the gun out of the man's hand. The man nursed his right hand with a grimace. The onlookers were surprised. Still nursing his painful hand, the man nodded at two other men who had been following them. The two men quickly disappeared behind a building.

By this time Longevity and Mai Mai had passed the Bella Union. The man with the black beard picked up his gun and entered the saloon. The crowd, laughing and shouting, began to disperse. A few followed the bearded man into the saloon.

"I did not know you could shoot like that, Longevity," Mai Mai whispered. "You are full of surprises."

"I did not know you could scratch like that," Longevity whispered back. "Let's go home."

"Aren't you having a good time?"

"No!"

"But I am!" Mai Mai said, and she resumed her mincing walk.

Longevity glanced at her and frowned. "Must you walk like that?" he whispered.

"I walk like a woman with small bound feet."

"But you don't have small bound feet."

"Can't I pretend? All my life—that's seventeen years—I wanted small feet. It's too late now, but who is to stop me from walking like a well-bred woman with a pair of three-inch bound feet?"

"My mother did not have small bound feet."

"She was a peasant woman."

"My father said that hundreds of years ago women with small feet were slaves. The Manchu Emperor wanted the Chinese to bind their feet so they could not run away."

"You told me that before. But men like them, don't they?"

"I don't. When I grow up I won't take a wife with small bound feet. A husband has to carry water for a wife with bound feet. And he can't hurry her up when she is slow in bringing the dinner."

"You will change when you grow up. At twelve you are only a small boy whose mouth still smells of his mother's milk."

"I'm thirteen!"

"You will change."

As they walked, they suddenly heard hoofbeats thundering from behind. "Look out!" Mai Mai cried. She tried to grab Longevity, but it was too late. Two men wearing sheepskin vests galloped by on horseback, knocking Longevity down. Longevity sprawled on the dirty street, his face bruised, his clothes splattered with mud and his gold nuggets spilling and scattering a few feet away from him.

"Gold!" a miner shouted.

The crowd scrambled for the gold. Longevity felt a sharp pain in his spine. Someone had pressed a heavy foot on his back, grabbed his pigtail and turned his face up. Longevity saw the large square face with the big black beard and smelled whiskey breath. "Where did you get all these nuggets, boy?"

"Yeah, where did you get them?" another man demanded. "You couldn't have made a strike so easy! Nobody is that lucky!"

"You stole them, didn't you, boy?" Black Beard asked.

"Gold thieves are worse than horse thieves! String 'em up!"

"Yes, string 'em up!"

"Where is the woman? Where is that China doll?"

"She escaped!"

"Let's string this one up! Somebody go get the ropes!"

"No, let's give him a fair trial!"

"What for? We string up horse thieves without a trial."

"Let's give him a fair trial and then string him up!"

By this time the man with the black beard had pulled Longevity to his feet and was marching him toward an oak tree in the square. A great many people gathered and followed them, shouting and arguing excitedly. Those who wanted to hold a trial were shouted down by the others. A few demanded that Longevity make a confession before the hanging. The man with the black beard ignored all the arguments and shoutings. He held Longevity by his collar and relentlessly marched him toward the oak tree. Another man came running with a coil of rope. The crowd was now getting wild. Some fired guns into the air. Others shouted, crying for blood.

Longevity began to drag his feet. The bruises on his face burned. He tasted blood in his mouth and felt cold sweat pouring down his back. The noises reminded him of the Chinese New Year. He closed his eyes tight and let Black Beard half push and half carry him; he tried to think of one happy New Year back home. It had been a good year. He was only five or six. There were a lot of firecrackers, and meat and fish for New Year's dinner.

Suddenly the wild shouting broke the spell. He realized where he was. He was going to die—to be hanged like those horse thieves Mr. Carnahan had caught. Somebody like Mr. King or Mr. Gordon was going to shoot him while he was dangling on a rope.

Then he thought of his father and felt like crying. Who was going to take his father's body back to China now? He did not mind becoming a wandering ghost himself, but his father, who had always wanted to be buried among the ancestors, would be heartbroken. His father's body would remain in that shallow grave in the wilderness forever without a tombstone, without a relative to make offerings or even to burn a few sticks of incense. "It is all my fault," he thought. "I have been an unfilial son. I have brought shame to the family name."

He opened his tear-filled eyes to see if Mai Mai was with him. All he saw was the big wild crowd. He saw the man with the beard. Another man was throwing a rope over a branch of the oak tree. Where was Mai Mai? Had she escaped? Was she kidnapped?

The crowd was getting wilder. The shoutings and firing of pistols tore at his nerves. It looked like a blood dance preceding an execution. He could even smell death now.

The man with the vest had successfully tossed the rope over the largest branch of the tree. Another man

213

stepped up, grabbed one end of the rope and proceeded to make a loop. The man with the big black beard was still holding Longevity and was busily shouting instructions.

Presently the crowd opened up and a horse appeared —a lively horse ridden by the other man who wore the sheepskin vest. The crowd shouted and cheered while the horse snorted and reared on its hind legs. The man got off the horse and brought it to the tree. He held the reins tightly, trying to calm the nervous animal.

Now the loop was made. Black Beard tightened his grip on Longevity. He pushed him closer to the tree with one hand and took hold of the loop with the other.

Longevity closed his eyes again. He wasn't afraid anymore. He only prayed for a quick death. He even felt faintly happy for he might see his father again. He felt the loop jerk under his chin. Then the rope tightened a little, almost choking him. He could smell Black Beard's breath and heard him shout, "All right, open up, men! Make way for the horse! We're ready to go. Open up!"

There was a big roar and the rope tightened again, almost raising Longevity off the ground. Just as he was about to be lifted onto the horse, he heard a woman's voice scream above the din, "Gold! Gold!" The screaming came closer. It silenced the wild crowd for a brief moment.

Longevity felt the rope slacken. He opened his eyes quickly. Miss Randall, covered with dust and her hair dishevelled, was breaking into the crowd. She frantically waved some gold nuggets in her hands and screamed, "Strike! Strike!"

One man grabbed her and demanded, "Where? Where, woman? Where's the strike?"

"East, man! Across the bay!" Miss Randall shouted. "Gold nuggets as big as eggs! Look!"

Longevity had never seen a mob disappear so fast. It was almost like a defeated army running for its life. In a few moments everybody was gone but Miss Randall and Mai Mai. Miss Randall gave the gold nuggets back to Mai Mai and quickly took the loop off Longevity's neck.

"Let's get out of here," she said, hustling Longevity toward a side street. "It's lucky Mai Mai had some nuggets for me to show to that mob. Otherwise nobody would have believed me."

"I'm sorry, Longevity," Mai Mai said. "I caused all this trouble."

"Hurry up!" Miss Randall said. "You can apologize to each other later."

Back in her cabin Miss Randall said to Longevity, "You have Mai Mai's fleet feet to thank. She came running faster than a horse."

Mai Mai smiled. "For the first time in my life I was glad I had big feet. You were not surprised that I am a woman, were you, Miss Randall?"

"No, I was not," Miss Randall said. "You Chinese always think we white people look alike. To tell you the truth, I've lived in China for twenty years and I still can't tell a Chinese woman from a Chinese man."

Longevity wanted to say something on this subject but couldn't. He was still choking with gratitude.

25

❦ When Mai Mai and Longevity told Number Nine of their secret mine and invited him to share the fortune and labor, Number Nine declined, saying that even nine horses could not drag him to the gold country. He reminded them about Three-fingered Jack, whose hobby was to string up Chinese by their queues. "There are better ways to die," he concluded, "such as falling into a well or overeating."

Mai Mai wondered if Miss Randall would be interested in joining them in their mining venture. Number

Nine's reaction was a horrified "No!" He said mining for gold was a gamble and Miss Randall abhorred gambling. Besides, Miss Randall did not need any gold; she had a wealth of it, right in her heart. "However," he added jokingly, "you would be lucky if you could get her to go with you. If Three-fingered Jack comes to enjoy his hobby, Miss Randall will grab his red beard and kick him in the shin with her iron-tipped shoes. She saved your life once; she might do it again."

"Shall we ask her anyway?" Longevity suggested.

"I have a suggestion," Number Nine said. "Come join me and Iron Head. There is plenty of gold in dirty laundry. Think it over."

They did not have to think it over. Longevity had to go and remove his father's body. While removing his father's body he might as well pick up the gold. Mai Mai agreed.

When they went to Miss Randall and extended their invitation, Miss Randall stared at them for almost a minute without saying a word. Longevity wiped his wet hands on his trousers; Mai Mai fidgeted, regretting that they had not listened to Number Nine. "Do you know?" Miss Randall finally spoke. "For fifteen years I have been trying to raise money for my missionary work in China. I think you two are God-sent. First things first. We will file the claim immediately. Go back and start packing. We will start for Sacramento without delay!"

Number Nine had just returned from work when Mai Mai and Longevity rushed back to pack. He wanted to cook a farewell dinner, but Mai Mai and Longevity did not have time. Then he brought out his homemade wine and everybody had a farewell drink. Mai Mai asked Number Nine if he was surprised that she was a woman.

"After I have seen Lotus Blossom chasing a donkey," Number Nine said, "nothing surprises me any more. But I am disappointed. For years I have wanted my wife to come and be the first Chinese woman in America. Now she will have to be the second. Bottoms up. To the first Chinese woman in America."

Longevity offered to pay for two months' lodging and food, but Number Nine wouldn't hear of it. He said his fellow countrymen should stick together, whether in luck or in distress. He illustrated his point by picking up a chopstick and breaking it easily, then he grabbed a handful, gave them to Longevity and told him to break them together. Longevity tried but couldn't. "See what I mean, fellow countrymen?" Number Nine went on significantly. "By sticking together we have strength."

Somewhat sadly, Mai Mai and Longevity left Number Nine.

Miss Randall filed the claim in Sacramento under the name "Charlie Luck." They hired a mule cart, bought two months' provisions for three people and started for the gold country without delay. Mai Mai remembered the trail well. They arrived at the hidden mine in the hills in two days. Mai Mai had avoided looking in the direction of Hangtown and the Chinese camp. But the more she tried not to think of Carnahan, the more she missed him. She missed the tents, the old oak tree in the square, the cabin in which she had swept floors, washed dishes, made coffee and shined boots. She wondered if Mr. King had killed Mr. Carnahan. The thought frightened her so much that she caught her breath and looked in the direction of Hangtown.

"Did you see a snake?" Longevity asked.

"I feel so rich now, I'm frightened," Mai Mai said.

"Never feel rich until you have the wealth in your pocket," Miss Randall said. "That's my philosophy."

Two months before, the fire had charred the hills. Now new trees and grass were sprouting. The grave was still intact, covered with weeds and wild flowers. They pitched a tent close to it and discharged the Mexican mule driver. Miss Randall wanted the mule cart, but knowing that the driver would ask a big price for it, she offered to buy the old mule for twenty dollars. The driver asked, "What will I do with the cart and no mule?" Miss Randall said he could sell it to her for two dollars.

Miss Randall spoke Spanish well, and told the driver that they had come to look for the site for a church. "Sorry to tell a lie," she said after the driver had left, "but in this case God will approve."

Then they removed Ta Ming's body from the shallow grave, packed it in a casket they had brought, and placed it under a young oak tree. Longevity kowtowed to it and made some offerings of food.

The mine proved to be rich and the digging easy. Nuggets as big as a man's thumb were imbedded like scrambled eggs in bluish clay. They dug them loose and sorted them as though they were picking wild strawberries. Mai Mai almost believed that the mine was some unknown emperor's secret treasure which had been buried before an enemy's invasion. Miss Randall said it was God's gift. Longevity did not have time to theorize. He was too busy digging. While not working, he sat beside his father's casket and admired the gold.

Longevity was the worrier. He worried about bandits and other miners who might come to jump the claim. But Miss Randall said that if the mine was God's gift there was nothing to worry about. God would see to it that the gold belonged to the right people. Besides, she had brought two shotguns, three revolvers, and sufficient ammunition to support the Lord's will. If undesirables invaded the mountain, she and Longevity could do the shooting and Mai Mai could load the weapons. Such teamwork would defeat an army, since they occupied the most strategic point on the hill.

In the evening, after work, Mai Mai would climb to the top of the hill, sit on a rock and look at Hangtown —or in the direction of Hangtown, which was well hidden behind a forest of oak trees in the distance.

When Longevity told Miss Randall what Mai Mai had been doing in her free hours, Miss Randall smiled. "Don't disturb her, Longevity," she said. "She is daydreaming, a habit of all girls her age. But it is God's design; nobody can help her. In time she will wake up, and find that dreaming is just as disillusioning as reality. Life is only interesting when you have a devotion."

"What is your devotion, Miss Randall?" Longevity asked.

"God. In God you find everything."

Although the mine was rich, the vein was small. At the end of seven weeks it was exhausted. On the last day of digging, Miss Randall tossed her pick down and wiped her brows for the last time. "That's it, children," she said. "Another hour of digging will bring us nothing but the sin of greed. We shall cook a nice dinner, say our grace to God and have a good night's sleep. Tomorrow we shall load everything on the mule cart and leave. We shall deposit our gold with Wells Fargo Bank in Sacramento, and ask the bank to transport it to San Francisco. Then we can all sleep in peace."

Mai Mai slept restlessly that night. At dawn, when they had loaded the coffin and the gold on the mule cart, Mai Mai asked Miss Randall if they could take a side trip to Hangtown and the Chinese camp for a short visit. She missed her fellow countrymen and wanted to know how they were doing.

"I don't see why not," Miss Randall said.

Longevity objected. He told Miss Randall that he had borrowed somebody's horse in Hangtown.

"We are rich now, Longevity," Mai Mai said. "We can pay for Mr. Carnahan's horse."

"Listen," Miss Randall said. "In this country you either buy a horse or steal a horse. There is no such thing as borrowing a horse. If you have stolen a horse you should pay for it and repent, then it will be a case of buying, not stealing."

"Longevity," Mai Mai said, "Mr. Carnahan won't hang you even if you don't pay him back. He is not like Mr. King or Mr. Gordon."

"Nothing to worry about," Miss Randall interrupted. "Since Longevity has survived the vicious mob in San Francisco, it's God's will that he will survive anything. Let's go, children, and trust your fate to God."

Once more Mai Mai made up like a coolie boy. On their way to Hangtown Miss Randall warned both of them not to brag about their gold. On the contrary, they should try to borrow money wherever they went. People then would avoid them like the plague. Before a bandit had a chance to level a gun at them, they should draw quickly, not with a gun but with this question, "How about a dollar for a bowl of chop suey?"

Miss Randall was not joking. She said that in these gold-crazy days it was the only way for a rich man to avoid danger. God was against lying, but He would sanction a little false hint if it was meant for self-protection.

Longevity trusted Miss Randall's wisdom and decided to follow it. Mai Mai was thinking about Mr. Carnahan. The possibility that Mr. King had killed him weighed heavily on her heart. As they approached Hangtown she found her throat dry and her heart pounding violently. "Mr. Carnahan can take care of himself," she told herself, determined to be cheerful. "Nothing will happen to him."

She also missed the villagers. She would like to greet them, ask Split-lip Lee about his good luck jade, Catfish Cheong about his savings, Chopstick Lew about his aches and pains. She would also pay Mr. Ling back for the paper money and incense she had borrowed for Longevity on the night of their escape.

Hangtown had changed. Most of the canvas tents were gone. The two permanent buildings were locked up. The only things that still looked the same were the oak trees. Even the largest one in the square was just as lush as before in spite of all Longevity's bullet marks.

Dozing on the bench in front of Mr. Carnahan's cabin was an old man with a snow white beard. Mai Mai stared at the cabin and swallowed hard a few times. "Go talk to him, Longevity," she said. "Ask him if Mr. Carnahan is in."

Longevity went forward and greeted the old man in English. The old man woke up with a start and quickly reached for his gun.

"What do you want?" he demanded.

Remembering Miss Randall's advice, Longevity asked to borrow a dollar. The old man dug out a small silver coin and tossed it at him. "Ain't much, but it'll buy you an apple, boy," he said.

"Where is Mr. Carnahan, sir?" Longevity asked.

"All gone. Carnahan, King, Gordon and that China-man. They say the diggings are better upstream. That's what they said about Hangtown a year ago. Now look at this place—a ghost town. Nobody here now but ghosts and landlords. I got stuck with three cabins. What are you doing here, boy?"

"I worked for Mr. Carnahan four months ago."

"Oh, yeah? More than a hundred Chinamen worked for him. He couldn't afford them. Couldn't even pay my rent. Hope the poor devil is doing better upstream. Where did you go, boy?"

"San Francisco."

The old man peered at him with a frown. "Didn't do too well there either, eh? Lots of you went upstream. Carnahan got jobs for them washing clothes for min-ers. A lot better than digging. Take my advice, boy, become a cook. You may ruin somebody's appetite, but you can always keep your own belly full while you're at it."

The old man squirted a mouthful of tobacco juice at a stone a few feet away and added, "Yeah, become a cook, boy." With a nod, he folded his hands and dozed off again.

Mai Mai felt sad but relieved. At least Mr. Carnahan was still alive. Seeing the cabin, she missed him more. "I wonder what happened to Mr. Quon," she said.

Miss Randall said there were only three things that could have happened to a gambler: he made a strike, he went bankrupt, or he got killed. "Wealth is distributed by God," she said. "Those who are entitled to it will be led to it by God's own hand."

Longevity felt bad about Mr. Carnahan and about his horse. Mai Mai suggested that they go upriver to find him. Miss Randall objected, saying that if a man deserved the loss of his horse, he would have lost it anyhow, either by gambling or to a real horse thief. Now that Longevity had made an honest effort to pay for it, his conscience was clear and he should consider the case closed.

Leaving Hangtown, Longevity contributed the old man's silver coin to Miss Randall for her missionary work in China. Miss Randall said it was a half-dollar and it would keep a poor Chinese family of five alive for a week. "Let's say a prayer for that old man," she said.

During the trip to Sacramento, both Mai Mai and

Longevity learned more about the foreign religion and went along with Miss Randall in all her prayers. And they said an extra grace to their own god, the Jade Emperor, for their gold.

They arrived in Sacramento like two peasant boys riding on a cart of hay. Miss Randall was driving. The mule cart jerked, bumped and squeaked on a muddy street that was teeming with miners, Indians, Mexicans and horses. Miss Randall pulled the cart to an abrupt stop in front of the Wells Fargo Bank. "Longevity," she said, "go into the bank and ask the president to come out. I want nobody but the president."

As Longevity hurried into the two-story brick building, Miss Randall pulled from under the hay a shotgun. She rested it in the crook of her elbow and scanned the street like an Indian scout, her eyes sharp and mouth a straight line, as if she were silently warning the crowds on the street, "All right, robbers, just try to rob me!"

Ordinarily a bank president wouldn't see a Chinese peasant boy, let alone come out at his bidding. But this one, a roly-poly Mr. Brown, was different. Only two weeks before he had heard that at Moore's Flat in the Yuba River District two Chinese had found a 240-pound nugget of gold worth over $30,000, which had been kicked about and overlooked by white miners. Four days later three other Chinese working a deserted claim on the Feather River found a three-hundred-pound nugget. They quietly chiseled it up into small pieces and sold it with their other gold dust without fanfare or the least bit of excitement. So Mr. Brown decided not to overlook the patronage of any Chinese, be he a boy or a man, a peasant or a Mandarin. He followed Longevity to the street.

"Are you the president?" Miss Randall asked as soon as the banker had stepped out of the building.

"Yes, Ma'am," Mr. Brown said, eyeing her and her cart of hay a bit suspiciously.

"Good," Miss Randall said. "I wouldn't deal with anyone but the top man." With that she cracked her whip and drove the mule cart right into the bank, to the consternation of the bank officials and many customers. Before the shocked bank president regained his composure Miss Randall leaped down from the cart, dusted her hands and apologized. "We've got some gold in the hay," she said. "It's safer to unload it inside. We want it shipped to San Francisco."

With the help of two guards, Mr. Brown found under the hay a coffin and a large old iron trunk. "It's in the trunk," Miss Randall said.

Longevity did not feel rich until the gold was properly weighed, assayed and deposited and a receipt had been signed by the president. According to the bank's calculation, the gold was worth a quarter of a million dollars. When Mr. Brown saw them off and smilingly shook their hands, he patted Longevity's pigtail a few times, saying it was for luck.

As they rode the stage coach back to San Francisco, Miss Randall said that the gold was a lot more than she had expected and that every cent of her share would go to God's two pet works: feeding the poor and saving souls in the Orient.

"And we have Longevity's filial piety to thank," she

added. "If Longevity had not feared for his father's body, we would not have become so rich. God likes you, Longevity. He would not take your hand and guide you to the gold, but He would put a little fear in your mind and let you do the rest. That's exactly how God conducts His affairs."

Miss Randall's comment made Longevity all the more anxious to take his father's body back to China and bury it properly among the ancestors. Miss Randall decided to go with him. Longevity asked Mai Mai if she would like to return to China.

Mai Mai wasn't listening. Since they had left the mines she had been thinking of nothing but Mr. Carnahan and wondering where he was.

"Ai, older sister," Longevity said, "why are you so dreamy-eyed? Are you thinking of what you can buy with all that gold?"

"What?" Mai Mai asked. "I didn't hear you."

Longevity nudged Miss Randall, who half guessed what was going on in the mind of the absent-minded young girl. "You should remain in this country, Mai Mai," she said. "So far as I know, you are the first Chinese woman ever to set foot in America. It would be a historical event—like Columbus' discovery of America—if you would settle down in California, marry one of the handsome Chinese bachelors and produce the first-born Chinese-American."

Miss Randall became quite excited about the idea as she talked about it. Longevity said Number Nine would make a good matchmaker, since he knew all the Chinese in San Francisco. Mai Mai wasn't interested in any of Number Nine's acrobatic friends. However, she blushed properly and retorted that Longevity was talking nonsense. "Aren't you thinking of a husband, older sister?" Longevity asked, nudging Miss Randall again.

"How do you know what I am thinking about?"

"Because half the time you do not hear me."

"I'm thinking of a hot bath and a good Chinese dinner."

"You should think of something more serious, older sister," Longevity said. Then he half jokingly reminded her that since he had become her brother, he wanted to be an uncle, too, so it was his duty to see that she married and produced many plump little babies.

"I hope you get married yourself," Mai Mai said vehemently. "Not to a nice woman, but to a big fat one who beats you twice a day for talking such nonsense!"

Miss Randall listened to them and chuckled. She could tell that Mai Mai did not really object to the idea. All her retorts were only a Chinese young girl's proper way to express her shyness. Miss Randall knew Chinese women very well.

26

❧ Number Nine and Iron Head had moved into new quarters in an area where no white men wanted to live because of fire hazards. In fact, the street had been destroyed twice by fire within six months and was now considered jinxed. Number Nine had told his partner that a white man's jinxed street might be a Chinese's lucky street. They had cleared the ruins and rubbish and built a four-room house with a lucky vermilion door. Other Chinese had followed suit and had put up shacks close by. The white men watched the industrious little men with curiosity and affectionately called them "China boys." Within two months the fire-devastated area became known as "Little China."

When Number Nine learned that Miss Randall had returned and had decided to go back to China, he gave a farewell dinner in her honor. He also took the opportunity to introduce to her some fellow countrymen who had just arrived from the gold country. He always welcomed his fellow countrymen to San Francisco and discouraged those who intended to leave for the gold country. There was plenty of gold everywhere in this land, he said, even in dirty laundry, so it was foolish to go dig gold in the wilderness and risk life and pigtail in the hand of Three-fingered Jack. If any fellow countryman hated to wash somebody else's dirty clothes, he could always go into the chop suey business. It was against his own conscience to fool the white man with such food, but if a cat preferred a dead rat to delicacies, that was its own business.

With the help of Iron Head, Number Nine prepared a nine-course dinner and invited everybody in Little China to the dinner party.

Miss Randall was delighted to see the Chinese community. She said that one of her great ambitions had been to build the first Chinatown in America, and now it was being built without any effort on her part. "The will of God," she concluded, and asked everybody to join her in saying grace.

When Number Nine's new friends arrived, Mai Mai immediately recognized all of them. Split-lip Lee, Catfish Cheong, Chopstick Lew and Mr. Ling were all there, thinner and darker, their pigtails well braided and their clothes newly washed.

When Mai Mai greeted them familiarly, they all looked bewildered, wondering who she was, a beautiful girl in a blue silk gown with long trousers covering her feet, a bright smile on her rosy-cheeked face.

"Don't you know me?" Mai Mai asked, highly amused.

Split-lip Lee screwed up his eyes trying to recall the "good old days" when he had been a man about town in the city of Canton. After a frantic search of his memory he couldn't honestly say that he had ever known any girl so young and pretty. But he wasn't ready to miss the opportunity to claim her as an old friend. He shot out a finger at her nose and exclaimed, "Ah, grind my bones into powder if you are not the famous Peach Flower of Canton!"

Mai Mai laughed.

Catfish Cheong decided that she was an entertainer provided by the host. Chopstick Lew stared at her, his mouth wide open, and made throaty noises like a famished man in a desert who had suddenly discovered a mirage.

Mr. Ling went a step closer and studied her with narrowed eyes as though he were studying somebody's vaguely familiar calligraphy, but couldn't make up his mind whose it was.

Longevity, getting impatient, stepped forward and told everybody who she was.

At first there was an expression of disbelief, followed by a chorus of oh's and ah's. Then finally Mr.

Ling flung out a long fingernail and exclaimed in a trembling voice, "Ah, Straw Sandal, I knew it was you!"

"Her name is Mai Mai now," Longevity said.

The greetings were friendly but reserved, as Straw Sandal was no longer a dirty coolie boy but a beauty whom everybody had ignored and even been rude to for almost a year.

Suddenly the men found themselves shy and ill at ease when they talked to her. Mai Mai enjoyed every moment of it, knowing how they felt. During the dinner she learned that Mr. Carnahan had quarrelled with Mr. King over an unknown woman, dissolved the company and gone upriver. Nobody knew what had happened to them. As for the villagers, about two dozen had come to San Francisco. The rest had scattered through the gold country, cooking, washing clothes, and doing other odd jobs for the white miners. Some had staked their own claims. Others had bought white men's deserted mines and were digging day and night. Among those who had come to San Francisco, Split-lip Lee decided to follow Number Nine's advice and operate a restaurant in Little China, which was being built on Sacramento Street. He had already started learning how to cook chop suey from one of Number Nine's acrobat friends.

Mr. Ling, never forgetting for a moment that he was a scholar, announced that he was going to set up a stall to write letters for those who could not read or write, with plans to expand his operation to fortune telling and studying people's horoscopes and physiognomy.

Chopstick Lew, who had come from a fishing village in China, was planning to establish a fish market selling clams; he would also sell spoons made of purple clam shells. He would put a few tables and benches outside his market so that customers could eat his clam soup with his clam spoons. "A stone for two vultures," he said. "That is how a man should think in business."

Catfish Cheong couldn't agree with him more. In fact, Catfish, who had once been a barber in China, had already started a multiple business on Sacramento Street. He kept a room in the back of his barber shop and installed in it a big iron bathtub. When he finished cutting a miner's hair he would say, "You dirty? You likee take bath? Lady she likee man smelly good. Good smelly bath four dolla."

Catfish Cheong had learned English from Number Nine and was using it to good advantage. Many miners would take a bath after the haircut and throw their dirty clothes away. The discarded clothes were Catfish Cheong's delight. He would pick them up, wash them, and sell them for a nice little profit. So Catfish was doing extremely well and he was already acting like a business tycoon and the unofficial mayor of Chinatown.

Catfish asked Longevity, somewhat patronizingly, what his plans were. Longevity announced his decision to go back to China. But he said he might return after he had properly buried his father, as his father had told him many times that there was more than gold in this foreign land.

Mai Mai was anxious to know more about Mr. Carnahan, but she asked about Mr. Quon instead.

"Mr. Quon has gone upriver with Mr. Carnahan,"

Catfish said. "Lost all his money. Wonder why he always follows that unlucky foreigner. I would not follow any man who went to pieces because of a woman."

"I agree," Split-lip said. "When he dissolved the company, I rubbed my lucky jade and said to myself, 'Never trust a man who fights over a woman!' "

"Wonder who that woman was," Mr. Ling said.

"Nobody has seen her," Catfish said, then added with a heavy sigh, "After Four-eyed Dog died, we all became blind and deaf. Nobody knew anything. Life at the camp was not the same anymore. *Wei,* Straw Sandal, uh, Miss Mai Mai, did you ever see a foreign woman in Hangtown?"

Mai Mai did not want people to know that she was the woman. "Yes," she said quickly, "I saw one foreign woman with yellow-colored hair. Big and tall. She would be laughed at in China."

"Most foreign women look like that," Catfish said. "Too much cow's milk. Eh, Split-lip, are you not glad you are Chinese?"

Split-lip shrugged. "Miss Mai Mai," he asked somewhat shyly, "what are your plans?"

"I am going back to China with Miss Randall and Longevity."

A few men groaned with regret. "Not me," Catfish said. "I am not going back until I have made enough money to buy a few acres of rice field."

"And a wife," Chopstick Lew said. "Don't forget that."

"Do you have to say that?" Catfish retorted. "When you buy fish, you don't talk about scales and bones. They come with the fish."

"Do you want a few concubines, too?" Mr. Ling asked.

Catfish laughed modestly.

"They are indicated in your physiognomy," Mr. Ling said. "You may learn the details in your horoscope."

The subject reminded Miss Randall of her new mission. Immediately after dinner she took Number Nine aside and asked him to make a match for Mai Mai. Number Nine said it wouldn't be difficult to marry Mai Mai off, even though she had large feet. He passed the word among his bachelor friends, who suddenly became more bashful, cast stealthy glances at Mai Mai and began to stammer.

Miss Randall studied them quietly, watched them talking and sipping Number Nine's fragrant jasmine tea nervously and made mental notes of each of them. She eliminated the ones whose mannerisms did not meet with her approval. She rejected Catfish, Split-lip, and Chopstick outright because of their names and looks. Mr. Ling was more dignified, but he was too old. She decided sadly that the selection was rather poor.

However, it was a successful dinner. Everybody was happy, especially the bachelors, who had not seen a Chinese woman for a long time.

27

❧ Although Mai Mai had given everybody the impression that she could hardly wait to go back to China, she secretly nursed the desire to find Mr. Carnahan. Having learned that there was no ship sailing for the Orient for one whole month, she suggested to Longevity that they take a final trip along the American River to bid farewell to their fellow countrymen. When Longevity hesitated, she added hastily, "Longevity, we are still guilty."

"Guilty of what?" Longevity asked.

"Guilty of stealing Mr. Carnahan's horse. I shall always feel unhappy unless we settle that debt."

"What do you want us to do?"

"Let's go find Mr. Carnahan and pay him for that lost horse. He won't hang us. He is not that kind of man."

"Where shall we look for him?"

"The upper American River. Isn't that what the old man told you in Hangtown? We shall buy two ugly shaggy horses in Sacramento and go find him."

"Why ugly shaggy horses? We can afford the best."

"We don't want people to know we're rich, do we? So, we shall ride ugly shaggy horses. Besides, nobody will suspect that we've stolen them."

Longevity, who loved horses and the gold country, and was pretty restless, agreed. After he had stored his father's coffin in Number Nine's back yard, he set out to find transportation with Mai Mai, who once more disguised herself as a boy.

San Francisco was becoming bigger and more prosperous. In Portsmouth Square they saw horsemen gallop about, and auctioneers cry their goods and ring bells to collect crowds. They heard brass bands playing with gusto in gambling saloons. And in the midst of all, runners and tooters for riverboats chanted their long-winded advertisements. One of them shouted at the top of his voice: "For two dollars you can ride up to Sacramento and all the way to the fabulous gold country, by the splendid steamer the *Golden Eagle,* the fastest boat that ever turned a wheel from San Francisco—with feather pillows and curled-hair mattresses, mahogany doors and silver hinges. She has got eight young lady passengers tonight, that speak all the popular languages. There will be no cardsharps from stem to stern, and the dice on board are not rigged."

After a short conference, Mai Mai and Longevity decided to take the boat instead of the stagecoach, which Longevity thought was too bumpy and hard on the seat. They bought two first-class tickets from the runner and boarded the *Golden Eagle* at Long Wharf. The boat was gaudily painted—a sidewheeler a little bigger than the first riverboat they had taken six months before. Their little cabin was on the upper deck, almost directly under the long, red-painted smokestack. Behind the pilot room on the bow was an open deck where many passengers milled about, mostly miners in red shirts and worn boots. There were a few well-dressed men in top hats, who leaned against the railings studying the other passengers. One of them, sitting on a portable card table, was shuffling a deck of cards.

Longevity examined the boat and found no silver hinges or lady passengers anywhere. In their little cubicle with the double bunk, he did not see any pillows either, let alone feather pillows, and the mattresses were hard and smelly. "Just try to believe the mattresses are stuffed with curled horse hair, Longevity," Mai Mai said philosophically.

"We must have some pillows," Longevity said.

Mai Mai pushed her luggage under the bunk. "Longevity, our sage has well said, 'A happy man still can be happy if he sleeps on thorns, eats galls for breakfast and uses his elbow for a pillow.' "

Both used their elbows for a pillow that night and

woke up the next morning with sleepy tingling arms. But they had a fairly good sleep in spite of the rough waters. The *Golden Eagle* did not stop tossing and rolling until it entered the Sacramento River Delta. Sailing on the calm river the passengers suddenly became alive again. The upper deck was crowded with people talking, laughing and gesticulating wildly. One man played a mandolin and a few others sang to his accompaniment in deep cracked voices. There were four card tables now instead of one, with the well-dressed men shuffling and dealing cards to the miners who surrounded them.

Ignored by the other passengers, Mai Mai and Longevity watched the activities, each preoccupied with a secret thought. Longevity admired some of the miner's clothes. He imagined himself to be one of the giant miners, growing a large bushy beard and wearing a red flannel shirt, with a flashy red scarf around his waist, a black leather belt beneath the scarf, fastened with a silver buckle from which hung a handsome six-shooter and a large bowie knife. He also wore a slouched, wide-brimmed hat, had a bold look that was a bit scary, and walked with a devil-may-care sort of gait. When he thought of all this he became very excited. He knew that he would grow big and tall, like his father, but he wasn't too sure that he could grow a large bushy beard. That was his only worry now.

Mai Mai had never stopped thinking of Mr. Carnahan, worrying and wondering. She had learned that the Mother Lode gold country covered a large area, that most miners worked along either the Feather River or the American River, which in turn had two important branches, the Upper Fork and the Middle Fork. She wished she knew where to look for him.

She wondered if Mr. Carnahan was on the *Golden Eagle*. It would be a miracle if he were. Many miners looked like him from a distance. But she ruled out the possibility by simply taking a glance at their boots. She had never seen any other man whose boots were so shiny and meticulously clean at all times as Mr. Carnahan's. She wandered around and glanced at people's boots. When she reached the pilot house she saw somebody who made her heart almost jump out of her mouth. It was Mr. King. She recognized immediately the deep-set, cruel eyes, the large bumpy nose with the sinking upper lip, and the long scar over his bushy eyebrows, which almost connected with each other as though they were one eyebrow instead of two.

Mr. King was the last man she wanted to meet again anywhere. Luckily he was busy piloting the boat, staring ahead into the river and puffing on a cigar. She quickly turned back and tugged at Longevity's sleeve.

Back at their cabin she told Longevity what she had seen. Longevity agreed with her that it would be dreadful if Mr. King knew she was aboard. They decided to stay in their cabin for the rest of the journey.

They got off in Sacramento as soon as the boat docked, bought two shaggy horses from a Mexican and immediately headed for the gold country. Their ugly horses were by no means slow. In fact they were so nervous and spirited that they had some difficulty in controlling them. Every time they tugged at the reins, the horses would jump and kick and snort. They almost galloped all the way to the upper Middle Fork of the American River.

Mai Mai and Longevity visited many mining towns and camps along the two forks, but could not find any trace of Mr. Carnahan nor any of the Chinese villagers they knew. Then they went to the Feather River. They had never seen so many mining communities with so many miners digging and hurrying about like ants on an ant hill. They inquired about Mr. Carnahan but most of the miners were too busy to talk to them. They visited most of the larger mining towns, and after two more weeks of futile search one helpful miner told them, "Forget it, boys. Nobody finds anything that's lost in the gold country, be it man or a wife or a horse. It's like trying to find a needle in a haystack."

As the Orient-bound clipper's sailing date drew nearer, they hurried back to Sacramento. Longevity had enjoyed the journey, especially the wild ride on the almost untamed horse. Mai Mai was reluctant to go back to San Francisco. She asked Longevity to find out if the *Golden Eagle* was in Sacramento. She was sure Mr. King knew where Mr. Carnahan was.

"Why are you so anxious to find Mr. Carnahan, older sister?" Longevity asked, looking at her askance.

"We owe him a debt of honor, Longevity. Don't we Chinese always pay our debts of honor?"

"Aw, I didn't know we Chinese were that honorable."

Grumbling a little, Longevity went to the Sacramento wharf and found a few idle ships, but the *Golden Eagle* was not among them. He inquired about it and was told that it had not returned for almost a month. Disappointed, they took the stagecoach back to San Francisco.

They found San Francisco changed again. The bay was crowded with ships of all kinds—sidewheelers, sternwheelers, lumber schooners, coasters, massive frigates, small fishing crafts, dinghies and launches. They rented a dinghy and searched for the *Golden Eagle*. Finally they found it rocking on the water not too far away from the dock. A bearded man with a broad, beefy face was hammering at something outside the pilot room. While Mai Mai waited in the dinghy Longevity went aboard and asked this man about Mr. King. The man spat some tobacco juice into the sea and said in a whiskey voice, "Never try to keep track of miners or riverboat pilots, boy. They are here today and gone tomorrow. Whenever there's a strike they all desert you." He flung an arm at the bay in a sweeping gesture. "See these ships? All deserted by their crews. For a month now I've been stuck with this bucket, sitting here like a dead duck, like all the others." He eyed Longevity with interest and asked, "Hey, boy, you look like an able-bodied man. You want a job?"

Longevity declined the offer with thanks and quickly returned to the dinghy. As they rowed away they heard the man spit and comment, loudly, "What's the world coming to? Even a doggone boy has turned down a man's job!"

They returned to Little China and found that even this little community had changed during their absence. More fellow countrymen had left the gold country and taken up trades. Besides restaurants and laundries, there was a poultry shop, with tier upon tier of shelves along the walls; imprisoned in bamboo cages on the shelves were lordly roosters, cackling hens and squawking white ducks, and one or two fat geese. Next to the poultry shop was a cobbler wearing a fur cap with ear muffs drawn down over his ears. He was busy heating his lead for soldering over a charcoal brazier. Across the street was a chair mender weaving thin strips of bamboo into broken seats. There were a few vegetable and art goods merchants ready to open for business. One was adding expenses on his abacus; others were hammering, hanging up signboards and painting doors. Everybody was busy building the first and the biggest Chinatown in America.

Number Nine's washhouse had become more prosperous. Many of his cousins had gone into the same business. He carried around in his inner pocket a clipping cut out from *Alta Californian,* the San Francisco paper. He would show it to every fellow countryman he met and read aloud to him the translation of the clipping, "Many China boys have gone into the laundry business. Much excitement was caused in the city last week by the reduction of washing prices from $8 to $5 a dozen. There is now no excuse for citizens to wear soiled or colored shirts. The effect of the reduction is manifest—tobacco juice bespattered bosoms are no longer the fashion."

Number Nine was very proud of the fact that he and his cousins had not only contributed to the cleanliness of the city, but had influenced the American fashion as well.

It came as a great disappointment and surprise to the

residents of Little China that Mai Mai meant what she said about going back to China. The common comment was that she did not really act like a Chinese woman, who was expected to point to east but look to west, or to say No but mean Yes or vice versa. However, on the day of her departure they all went to the dock to see her off.

It was a fine day. The trim clipper, *Flying Cloud,* docked at Long Wharf, was shiny with new white paint. The fog in San Francisco Bay lifted early. The sun was warm and the water calm. Seals sunned themselves peacefully on the rocky islands that dotted the beautiful bay. Seagulls glided around the clipper and cried excitedy, as though to bid the ship farewell.

Longevity, wearing a new silk gown and flanked by Mai Mai and Miss Randall, waved goodbye to his friends. His father's body, packed in the expensive casket, had already been stored in the ship's stateroom.

"Longevity," Number Nine called from the dock, "take good care of your older sister."

"You know I will," Longevity shouted back. "When I return you will find that I have already become an uncle."

Mai Mai blushed and stamped her feet with pretended annoyance. "Oh, you all speak such nonsense," she retorted loudly for everybody to hear. "How disgusting!"

The bachelors liked it. This was a well-bred girl who knew how to conduct herself in public. They felt more sorry than ever that she had to go. "Come back, Longevity!" they all shouted.

244

Mai Mai looked at the hilly land sadly and wondered if she would ever see it again. Where was Mr. Carnahan now? Had Mr. King killed him? No, she could not believe that he was dead. Was he still in the mines? If he was, had he made a strike? She must not think about him. She was rich now; she must make plans for her future. First, where would she live? Not Heavenly Tranquillity. Perhaps she and Longevity could go into business together. They could open a dress shop, or buy a lot of houses and become landlords. She would not marry until Longevity was old enough to take care of their business.

She wondered what had happened to Mooncake Quon. Perhaps she should find him and give him a job. He was a bright boy. But she could not love him again. He was too young. One day she would meet a man like Ta Ming, a real man, handsome, decisive, commanding, and very serious about things. She would treat Mooncake like a brother. When the time came, she would choose a wife for him. Mooncake could live in a house in the back of hers. She wasn't sure Mooncake would like to be the manager of her dress shop; perhaps he could collect rent for her and Longevity. It did not take special skill to collect rent. Mooncake could do it. He was friendly. His only shortcoming was that he wasn't stubborn. She could see him collect rent for her now. "Come tomorrow," the tenant would say. Mooncake would be firm at the beginning. "It's due," he would say. The tenant would say, "What's the difference? Money doesn't grow old." Perhaps the tenant didn't have money; perhaps he had six daughters whom he wanted to marry off. Wouldn't it be interesting if Mooncake went there many "tomorrows" and wound up marrying one of the tenant's daughters?

She smiled at the thought. Mooncake was the kind of easygoing boy who would do a thing like that. Longevity would like him. They could become brothers, or brothers-in-law. The tenant might have a daughter who was Longevity's age.

She became faintly excited as she thought about all these possible developments. Suddenly she saw a man in a red shirt and shiny boots working among the stevedores on the dock, busily unloading a large mule cart of wooden crates. She stared at him, her heart pounding. She recognized the erect gait, the swift movement and the agility. Even working as a stevedore he showed grace and style.

Without a word she dashed ashore. She heard Longevity's voice calling, *"Wei, wei,* older sister, where are you going? The ship is sailing!"

She ran toward the man and stopped about thirty feet away from him. Yes, it was Carnahan, darker and thinner, like all the others from the gold country; but he was still clean and handsome, doing three men's jobs among those slow and clumsy men. He stared at her, stunned. Why was he so surprised? Was it because of her new looks? Was he glad to see her? "Hello, John," she said somewhat fearfully.

Carnahan came to her, his steps slow but sure, like those of a cat approaching its prey. He looked serious, still staring at her with utter disbelief. But when he came closer she could see the sparkle in his deep-set green eyes, and his serious expression was about to break into a smile. "What are you doing here?" he asked. It was the same voice, deep and clear and commanding.

"I'm going back to China," she said. "I've come to say goodbye."

She didn't expect him to kiss her but he did. They clung to each other, unashamed and oblivious to all the others on the dock. Some stared, some laughed, some came closer like the crowds at Portsmouth Square gathering to watch a medicine show.

She was too happy to say anything. But she must say something; time was running short. "John," she asked, "did you have a missing horse?"

"Missing horse? What missing horse? I had a sweating horse one morning. Why did you leave me?"

"Because I afraid. Mr. King kill you. So I leave. No more trouble."

"So you took the horse."

"Yes," she said.

"Lucky it was my horse, and it came back. You know how they treat horse thieves in the gold country."

"You still can string me up."

"I would. Not for stealing my horse, but for breaking my spirit. I wasn't the same man anymore after you left."

"You still the same."

"What? A stevedore?"

"You still the same."

Carnahan smiled. "You still the same, too. Your ship has sailed."

Mai Mai turned and looked. The clipper had left the dock, moving slowly toward the bay. Seagulls were circling the white shiny sails, screaming. Mai Mai made a dash toward the water but Carnahan grabbed her. "It's too late now," he said.

She had expected Carnahan to grab a boat and row her to the ship, yelling for it to stop. But he didn't. What he had done cleared all her doubts. She wanted to confess that she didn't want to leave the Land of the Golden Mountain anyway, but she couldn't. "Yes, too late," she said, feigning disappointment. "I take next ship."

Carnahan didn't say anything. He tightened his grip on her arms as though he was afraid of losing her again. They looked at each other for a moment, then clung to each other again, refusing to let go. For the first time she felt she belonged, and the feeling was so wonderful. She wondered what Number Nine and the other Chinese were doing. Oh, she didn't care, really. She and Carnahan were together now. That was important; nothing else mattered.

She glanced in the direction of the ship. It was sailing farther away from the dock now. Then she saw something that made her catch her breath. Split-lip Lee and Catfish Cheong were coming toward her with a heavy chest—her brand new iron chest with two locks, in which she had packed her gold and her clothes. She had completely forgotten about it.

The two men put the chest down a few feet away from her and greeted Mr. Carnahan, who returned the greeting in Cantonese.

"Longevity thought you might need your clothes," Split-lip said, wiping his brows and rolling his eyes. "He asked us to bring you this."

"Heavy, heavy," Catfish said after a deep breath. "Must be full of gold."

Mai Mai choked with gratitude. She buried her face in Carnahan's shirt and cried.

On the *Flying Cloud* Miss Randall watched Mai Mai enviously with a smile, her stubby fingers smoothing the enormous watch that was hanging from her neck on a chain.

"I'll be damned, I'll be damned," Longevity said. "Whenever she smiled that dreamy smile, I always thought she was thinking of a roast chicken. Who could know it was Mr. Carnahan?"

"You were thoughtful to send her the luggage," Miss Randall said. "And I've forgiven you for swearing because of it."

"Miss Randall," Longevity asked, "how did you know she would not come back?"

"All horses return to their stables. All girls in love go back to their men. It's the design of God, Longevity. Let's go in and wash up for dinner. We'll say a prayer for both of them at the dinner table."